Hotel Lamia: Where Immortals Sleep

Tiffany Ann

Publisher Tiffany Ann

www.tiffanyannbooks.com

ISBN: 9798487106247

Table of Contents

Dedication

I dedicate this story to everybody who has passed through my life in the hotel industry. We have the best life stories to tell.

Thanks to my work friends, old and current, who I hang out with. Dinner, drinks, and game nights are the best with you guys. Whitney, Chris, and April, I think I laugh the most when we are together. Life may eventually send us our separate ways, which I dread, and if that happens, I will never forget you.

To Trudy, I imagine we are forever friends, after all we've been through together. At least I hope so.

To Ai, I miss working with you. It's not the same without you. I hope Blake treats you well for all your days.

To Mitzi, who is hundreds of miles away now, but read my books and recommended them. I was in awe of your support. Miss you.

To Winter, whose comment: "Please tell me there's more of that. Because it was crazy. It's one of those books I just want to throw myself on the floor and process what I just read. Lmao. I freaking love it," is still the best response so far.

And to my boss, whose name I won't mention for business privacy reasons. Thank you for taking a chance on somebody who hadn't worked in thirteen years and didn't have any experience in hospitality. I love my job, and the perks that come with it.

Special Thanks

I want to thank my husband, **Allen,** who listens to me ramble on about my books without complaining. I couldn't have described the settings without your skill. I love you more than you know.

My oldest daughter, **Brianne,** I must mention that some of Nicole's sayings are my daughters who wouldn't want me taking credit for them.

Julie, thank you for being a sounding board, and inspiring me to step out of my comfort zone to write a story about vampires. As much as I love human, I had so much fun writing this story.

To **Jenna O'Malley,** author of *Bound by Fate and Blood.* Your honesty regarding passive voice opened my mind in ways I struggled with before. There have been times I stared at the screen, when the editing program suggested using an active verb instead of passive and I couldn't find the words to change it and express what I wanted to say. Going through this writing when editing, it lit up like a Christmas tree where I used passive and then the action verbs now slammed me in the face with ideas to turn it into that action. I'm sure I have a long way to go to improve, but it's a start. Thank you for the push and encouragement.

I can't forget all my **beta readers**. Thank you for your faithful continued support with each book.

Thank you to **Best Book Editors** for all your tips and suggestions. I grew so much as a writer working with you.

Thank you to **Connie B. Dowell** for the second round of edits. Finding you to work with is a dream come true. You make it so easy.

*Warning-this book contains a good bit of foul language and explicit scenes. *

Introduction

I've always loved a good vampire tale, but I would roll my eyes over some myths surrounding vampires. And that is the inspiration for much of this novel.

This is a story based on what I imagine the world would look like if vampires were real.

My story is fiction. However, many of the hotel stories are based, in part, on my life as a front desk night auditor.

My co-workers and I exchange stories each shift change, and they joke about how I need to put these moments in my books. I took their advice, and what you read in these pages is my best portrayal of the hilarious instances we encounter. Not everything you read is true.

I hope you enjoy my mythological vampires as they own and operate a supposedly haunted hotel named after the vampire-like goddess Lamia.

Prologue

There are varying stories regarding the death of Judas Iscariot. You may have heard the account according to the apostle Matthew, "Then Judas, which had betrayed him, when he saw that he was condemned, repented himself, and brought the thirty pieces of silver again to the chief priests and elders, saying, 'I have sinned that I have betrayed innocent blood.' And they said, 'What is that to us? See thou to that.' And he cast down the pieces of silver in the temple, and departed, and went and hanged himself."

Or you may have heard the apostle Peter's speech in Acts, "Men and brethren, this scripture must needs have been fulfilled, which the Holy Ghost by the mouth of David spake before concerning Judas, which was guide to them that took Jesus. For he was numbered with us, and had obtained part of this ministry. Now this man purchased a field with the reward of iniquity; and falling headlong, he burst asunder in the midst, and all his bowels gushed out."

Which account is accurate? Maybe neither. Maybe both. Possibly, Judas Iscariot attempted to hang himself, but the limb broke, sending him headlong into a field beneath the tree. And it's possible that he might have received a visit in the field from

Lucifer.

Lucifer, the master of deception and trickery, asked Judas, "Did the Son of God say to you, 'Woe unto that man. It had been good for that man if he had not been born'?"

Judas replied in anguish. "He was right. It's true. I should never have been born."

"If that were true, why did the limb snap instead of your neck? Why are you still laying here in this hole in one piece?"

"Because death is too merciful."

"Ah, so what if I offer you something other than death?"

Judas looked at Lucifer for the first time, his curiosity piqued.

When he didn't respond, the master deceiver continued. He pulled a piece of fruit from behind his back and offered it to Judas. "Do you know what this is?"

After examining the fruit carefully, he shook his head.

"I picked it from the *Tree of Life* before He kicked me out of the garden. Eat this and you will never die."

Looking at the decayed fruit, Judas asked in confusion, "How is that worse than death?"

"Eat this and it will curse you to walk the earth for all eternity. You will escape the fires of hell. You will never see the gates of heaven. Your curse will be to live in the same body, with the same soul, never to escape the pain and suffering of this world. Your God didn't close the garden to punish humans. He hid the *Tree of Life* and guarded it, because the only fate worse than death is immortality on this planet. Night after night. Day after day. And it never ends."

Lucifer extended his hand with the rotten piece of fruit toward Judas, who snatched it from his hand, eating the entire piece in one bite.

When the juices of the fruit hit his stomach, Judas's body convulsed. He foamed at the mouth, blood poured from his ears, eyes, and nose. He fell to the floor and spasmed, his body convulsing in a rictus brought on by the poison. There was no reprieve from the torment his human form endured until he spilled every drop of his mortal blood.

Lucifer impatiently waited for Judas's body to finish. When he lay there as though dead, Lucifer spoke the last words of the curse. "You will no longer walk in the day, and are cursed to live in the dark. You will no longer only eat from the table or drink from the vine. Henceforth, you will crave the blood of the innocent. You will not walk this earth alone in your immortality. One day others will seek you out, asking for your curse. There is but one way to end your penance, and that is to attempt to pass it to somebody against their will. The curse will cease, and so will you. Your body and soul—no more. There will be neither a place for you in heaven nor in the depths of hell."

As the deceiver descended back into hell, he said, "You are no longer Judas Iscariot. Choose a new name."

Judas whispered his name to the wind, "From now on, they will know me as Dracula."

History of Hotel Lamia, New Orleans, LA

Hotel Lamia is one of New Orleans' best-kept secrets. Few enter the obscure building, thinking it abandoned. The *Unwelcome* sign might deter the fainthearted.

It was once the home of Madame Céleste Bourgeois in Storyville, where prostitution was legal. Opened in 1897, Madame Céleste and her girls serviced men from all walks of life. The elite, politicians, tourists, and others walked through her doors, looking to fulfill their wildest fantasies.

In 1909, one of Céleste's working girls was found murdered in her bed by another of the girls—strangled with a scarf. It's believed her ghost haunted the brothel for a year, seeking revenge.

In 1910, a fire broke out. Witnesses claimed the flames took on an unholy manner, engulfing the building faster than naturally possible. The fire took the lives of everybody inside, including the suspected murderer, trapping their spirits inside the walls. The rumors say—if they speak the truth—over fifty souls wander the halls of Hotel Lamia. Some claim to hear their screams at night.

Bought and restored by the Nikoli family shortly after the fire, the hotel has been in their lineage for more than a hundred years.

Are you brave enough to stay the night in a place where screams shake the walls each night? Where ghosts watch you slumber, slipping in and out of your room throughout the night?

Named after the vampire-like Greek goddess Lamia who fed on the blood of children, Hotel Lamia promises an unforgettable stay. It's guaranteed that every guest will leave with a scream on their lips and a story to tell. If you survive the night, what will yours be?

The humans are told the watered-down version of events, while the vampires take advantage of their gullible nature.

Immortals seek a place to lay their head during the day. Behind the doors of Hotel Lamia, they know there's a private source to satiate their need for blood.

With the promise of blood under contract, they leave the donor alive and unharmed, or they may face the ultimate punishment.

Chapter 1 ~ Kovac

Kovac isn't the name his parents gave him at birth. It was the name he took for himself as a cursed being. When his maker gave him the choice between eternal damnation in the fires of hell or eternal damnation to walk the earth immortal, it seemed a simple choice.

Born in Moravia over one thousand years ago, his maker found him with an arrow in his gut, pleading to the gods that he wanted to live. The Magyars crossed the Carpathia Mountains on horses, bringing death and terror in their wake, and Kovac fell victim to them.

His homeland—no longer known as Moravia. The history of his country had changed so many times over the last thousand years that he didn't know what to call it—or how to find it. His best guess was that it was located in the country he knew as the Czech Republic. An internet search might shed some light on the subject. Not that he cared. He left that part of his life behind and never looked back. The words of his native tongue no longer lingered on his lips. A forgotten memory of the human life he abandoned.

Cursed to live a never-ending life of pain, loneliness, and heartache. A life without parents, siblings, children, or grandchildren. An existence without family meant he lived to survive and nothing else. Like all immortals, a life fulfilled did not exist for him.

The first vampire chose the path of immortality, for death was not punishment enough for his sin. Most chose vampirism because they feared death and the unknown. Some chose it knowing hell awaited them for their crimes.

Kovac became a vampire because death terrified him. Because of his childish fear, he doomed himself to a vicious endless cycle. The only escape would be through turning somebody against their will. The punishment—instantaneous oblivion. He would cease to exist. If he hadn't chosen the path that looked brightest, he might have gone to heaven. He hadn't been a bad person before the arrow struck him. He'd never know what destiny originally planned for his eternal life.

At first it was all fun and games. He moved faster, his muscles were stronger, his senses heightened, and he didn't age. His inability to age after a decade forced him to leave the people he loved and to never look back.

He'd fallen in love on more than one occasion. Most vampires turned their lover, but Kovac could never bring himself to ask the women he loved to bear the curse. He loved them too much, so he left without saying goodbye as soon as they noticed that he wasn't aging.

His home of choice these days was the French Quarter in New Orleans, Louisiana. He owned Hotel Lamia with another vampire—his best friend. They called themselves brother and sister for propriety's sake.

Searching for a name that struck terror in the hearts of those who dared entered, they chose Lamia for her vampire-like qualities and because in some cultures they referred to her as the boogeyman in order to scare children into behaving.

They bought and repaired hotels notoriously noted for their hauntings. Kovac had never encountered a genuine ghost in his millennia. A haunted hotel, though, was the perfect cover for vampire feedings, which is why they owned several across the world. From Paris to Mexico and seven other locations spread out around the globe. Every decade or so, they'd switch hotels to keep the locals from questioning their static appearance.

Each room connected to an adjoining one. A vampire rented the connecting room of every guest. Guests came from far and wide to live the tales they'd heard about the hotel.

The vampire guest had a key to the adjoining room, and would sneak into the human's room at night. Sometimes they were asleep, sometimes awake. It didn't matter, because a vampire's venom heals the puncture wound and leaves no evidence.

Most guests waved the encounter off as a bad dream when they woke up alone and unharmed. Others believed ghosts came to them at night. Some were convinced of the truth, but lacking proof, it remained myth and legend to the outside world.

Kovac enjoyed the stories his guests told every morning of things that went bump in the night. They were his only moments of pleasure.

Loneliness spilled from deep in his soul, all the way out through the pores of his skin. Having another to share his existence with consumed his every thought, but he would never turn a human being into what he was.

Chapter 2 ~ April

April was not the name given to her by her parents; it was the name she chose for her immortal life. In her three hundred-plus years as a vampire, the question always asked was, "Were you born in April?"

"Nope."

"Then why did your parents' call you April?"

"They didn't. I chose the name just to fuck with people who ask stupid questions."

April had a foul mouth, and her best friend and business partner, her brother to the human world, Kovac, insisted she keep her language under control when dealing with guests. She only respected his request because she owed him more than she could ever repay. However, in her personal time, it was a different story, and she could say whatever she liked.

She was a human destined for hell. It was something that had never bothered her until she lay in a pool of her own blood. Why she suddenly called out for an alternative to hell was still a mystery.

April hated people, especially after her lover had

abandoned her when she turned immortal. Humans annoyed the shit out of her. Yet she was destined to spend all eternity surrounded by people.

Maybe in hell, she would have had a private corner to burn in for all eternity. She'd made her choice and now she'd never know. Fear caused idiots like her to make stupid decisions in the heat of the moment.

Sitting at the front desk—working her shift, and listening to another human bitch about housekeeping—she wondered how in the world she'd let Kovac talk her into working in customer service.

The answer was simple. He was the only being she'd ever come across that she could tolerate. If it wasn't for Kovac, she'd have ceased to exist when her bloodlust and ignorance nearly caused her to try to turn someone without their consent.

Her maker turned her and left her on her own before she even awoke immortal. Turning someone was a tremendous responsibility. One most didn't take lightly. To turn someone, you took on the role of a parent or mentor until the new vampire could control themself on their own.

A new vampire's instinct was for blood at any cost. Self-control had to be taught. The vampire laws had to be drilled into their heads, or they would face entombment from vampire hunters.

Being immortal, hunters couldn't kill vampires with fire, stakes, holy water, or beheading. All of that was myth. They could entomb captured vampires, which was a fate worse than oblivion. Entombed, they buried the vampire alive. Without blood, the addiction withdrawals were constant and eternal.

Unless a vampire violated human laws, like murder, the hunters left them in peace. If not for Kovac, April would have killed a human and been punished by hunters, or worse.

Kovac found her in an alley about to offer her blood to her partner in her human life. They were as notorious and fearless as Bonnie and Clyde when she lived as a mortal. Her fearlessness nearly killed her. Except her Clyde rejected her in the end. Going out in a blaze of glory for the woman he loved wasn't part of his plan. He turned on her when she told him what she had become. April overpowered him and planned to force him to spend eternity with her. Being left on her own, she didn't know what the consequences were, and she didn't care.

Kovac stopped her. He saved her, taking the role of her mentor. She had been with him ever since. Leaving him to pursue her dreams was not an option—not while he was alone. That is the reason she agreed to be a co-owner of Hotel Lamia.

There were perks to owning their hotels. She could wear what she wanted, which was usually a t-shirt with a smartass comment on it. As long as it didn't include a cuss word on it, Kovac didn't fight her on wearing them behind the front desk.

Tonight's t-shirt said, *Sorry, honey. Sarcasm falls out of my mouth, just like stupid falls from yours.*

To keep with the haunted vibe, they only required housekeeping to clean the bathroom facilities, change the sheets, and vacuum the floors. The dust, cobwebs, and bugs were part of the hotel's amenities. It was in the brochure and on the website. Yet she sat, listening to another idiot who failed to read the listing. She rolled her eyes in frustration enough times that he should have decked her before he finished complaining.

Kovac would have politely said something like, "We regret you overlooked the description of our hotel. Would you like to take your business elsewhere?" He might have even offered a refund.

Not April. "Let this be a lesson for you. Always read the fine print," she told the brainless human before getting up and leaving the front desk. She never stuck around to make the guest happy. It was pointless, because it didn't matter what she said. They would find something else to moan about.

She found Kovac in the office, going over the books. "Pissed off another guest?" he asked when she walked in with her usual attitude.

"I'm done. I'm just done." She spit out the same words she told him every week before mumbling her usual comment under her breath. "Idiots."

The first thing she liked about Kovac when they met—he didn't ask her why she chose the name April. He was the one who told her she had to choose a new name. The second thing she liked about him: he never asked her to be someone she wasn't.

They were night and day. Polar opposites. Opposites usually attract, but their relationship wasn't like that. They were attracted to each other like magnets, but not romantically. They were family, not by blood, but by choice. Kovac loved her and was there for her more than her blood family ever was.

He respected her no-nonsense attitude and even wished he had it in him to act more like her sometimes. April respected his ability to care and always see the best in people. On rare occasions, she wished she had even a touch of his compassion.

The bell at the front desk rang, pulling her out of her thoughts. She dragged herself away from the office to help the next moron to walk through their doors.

Chapter 3 ~ Nicole

Since Nicole's diagnosis, she'd roamed the country far and wide. She was uncertain about what she hoped to find during her last days.

The many doctors she consulted recommended chemotherapy to prolong her life, but that was all it would do, give her a small window of time. Living her last days hooked up to machines, and being pumped with poisons while her friends and family wept over her wasn't what she wanted.

Stepping off the train in New Orleans, her soul pulled her in the city's direction. Her feet walked as if they had a mind of their own. Being unfamiliar with her surroundings, she followed her feet without question.

It was only about a mile later she found herself outside of a hotel in Storyville. Storyville was known for debauchery, drunkenness, gluttony, and the like. At one time, prostitution had been legal here.

The three-story building looked like something out of a horror movie. At first glance, it seemed abandoned, but somebody came out of the building, proving she should never trust first impressions.

Nicole ran her hand along the gray plastered wall, covered in ivy. Her fingers danced with delight as they dragged along the rough finish.

A raised wooden paneled gothic door had been left to the elements and looked worn and tattered, making it a darker shade than the walls. She could see broken remnants of glass in the arched transom above the door frame. The antique brass Bergerac door handle beckoned her. She stared at the door, feeling a gnawing sense of longing in her heart. Despite the distressed sign next to the door saying, *Unwelcome,* Nicole Ripp felt she belonged on the other side.

She reached for the handle, and before her fingers could wrap around the metal pull, the door opened on its own. Creaking sounds filled the entryway. To many the sounds screamed, *beware* and *danger,* but she saw *welcome, come on in.*

She stepped through the front door, sensing in her heart this was her final resting place.

In the lobby, a black leather sofa sat in the center, with matching armchairs on each side. Furniture lined the walls, covered in white sheets. Based on the shape of the sheet tossed over the pieces, there had to be a piano underneath it.

The dark, damask wallpaper hung worn and forgotten. It peeled off the walls as if placed up on the walls decades ago and never given another thought.

It was so dark in the reception area, despite a gorgeous, antique, brass chandelier with crystal medallions hanging from the water-stained, domed ceiling, but it was missing several bulbs. Dusting was obviously not something housekeeping found the time to do. Layers of dust had formed on the chandelier and cobwebs decorated the once ornate plaster crown molding, outlining the ceiling of the grand entryway.

Nicole wondered why anyone would choose to stay there,

yet she had no intention of leaving.

A young woman stood behind the front desk wearing the rudest shirt that said, *Sorry, honey. Sarcasm falls out of my mouth, just like stupid falls from yours.* Nicole chuckled when she finished reading it.

The woman had a messy, layered, short haircut dyed bright pink, or maybe it was a wig, she concluded after closer inspection. She had eyes that were as black as night, outlined with black eyeliner, thin red lips, and beautiful high cheekbones. She stood shorter than Nicole by a couple of inches.

Nicole walked right up to the woman and said, "I wish I was brave enough to wear a shirt like that."

Her statement earned her a smile from the stranger. It was an awkward smile, as if the woman was unaccustomed to smiling.

"What can I do for you?"

"I guess—I'll take a room."

"Just for one night?"

"Can I start with a week?"

"You can, but I warn you, most barely make it through one night."

"I'm not most people." Nicole didn't know where her confident declaration came from because she was exactly like most people in many respects. The exception was that in this place that ought to scare her to her bones, she felt peace.

The woman offered her another smile while checking her in for a seven-night stay.

The key to her room reminded her of an antique skeleton key. She hoped it wasn't an original skeleton key that would allow anyone to enter her room.

The hand-operated elevator had a sign posted outside, reading *out of order,* so she had to take the stairs to the third floor. The handrail appeared to be hand-carved cypress wood with ornate, wrought iron spindles and balusters. Her hands slid easily along the beautiful architecture on her way to her room. At least she had little luggage to carry up the three flights, just the backpack on her back.

Chapter 4 ~ April

April finished checking in the second person in the world that she liked on first impression. "I just met the perfect woman for you," she told her best friend.

Looking up from his paperwork, Kovac gave her his full attention. "Are you trying to set me up again?" He rolled his eyes at her.

"I know you want someone to share eternity with, and maybe she's the one."

"I desire eternal companionship, but you know I won't curse anybody else like this. Especially not someone I love."

"One day, you might. I put her in the room next to yours. She booked seven nights, and if you're interested, her name is Nicole Ripp."

Kovac shook his head at her attempts to bring him joy in this miserable life he chose. Returning to his paperwork was his way of telling her the conversation was over.

"Well, I like her. And I only like you, so you should at least pay her a visit before you ignore me," April told him on her way back to the front desk, ensuring she had the last word on the subject.

Stubborn moron. Out of respect, the thought remained in her head. If anyone deserved happiness in this world, it was Kovac.

According to myths and legends, vampires didn't have a soul. Which idiot came up with that? A soul is your mind, will, and emotions. If a vampire didn't have one, they would be mindless blood sucking zombies. Sure, many vampires lost their conscience, but never their soul. It was part of the eternal curse. Their bodies weren't even dead, like the stories claim. A dead body develops rigor mortis, blood stops flowing, their heart stops beating, and so on. Since they weren't dead, probably more like undead, their soul was still very much alive.

Kovac's conscience never left him, and the chances of him ever losing it were slim. His conscience kept April from throwing hers away. He was her Jiminy Cricket.

April's joy in her miserable existence came from saying whatever the hell she felt like saying. Knowing she could kill anyone who didn't like it especially helped. Even though the only time she killed anyone was in her mortal life.

Kovac only experienced happiness when he had someone to love, but it was always short-lived, since he refused to turn anyone.

She made it her mission in life to find someone to bring Kovac a bit of peace on this planet. Until then, she was stuck with him.

Traveling, never staying in one place for long, was the life April wanted, the life she had before she turned, but until Kovac found eternal love, she wouldn't abandon him.

Another guest walked in the front door and with a pesky, stinky dog.

"We're not pet-friendly, sir." April faked politeness.

"It's my service dog," he told her.

"Well, I can't turn you away, but we have a disclosure regarding animals." She pointed to the sign, *Warning, animals never survive the night.*

"What does that even mean?" the moron with the cheap toupee asked her.

"We don't have a reasonable explanation, but every guest who brings a pet into this facility wakes up to find their animal dead," April coldly told him, knowing full-well he wouldn't believe her.

"You just say that to scare guests from bringing pets. It's not actually true."

April didn't dignify the stupid man with a response. She had warned him, and if he wanted to risk it, that was on him. The poodle, which its owner had dyed blue, was probably a comfort pet and not a service animal. It would be her dinner, and his owner her dessert. She unapologetically handed him a room key next to her suite.

Chapter 5 ~ Kovac

April's suggestion about the woman in the room next to his suite called to him, as it always did. He desired eternal companionship more than he had feared death that day on the battlefield. If only it didn't require him to trap someone's soul in their body for eternity, he could have a lasting love like everybody else.

He'd searched the world for most of his one thousand years as a vampire, hoping to fall in love with another vampire, but too many had thrown their conscience away. Kovac was an anomaly whose conscience grew stronger with each passing year.

A pint of blood was sufficient sustenance in one hit, yet many gorged, leaving their victim dead, aware vampire hunters might catch up with them one day.

One reason he opened his hotels was his need to save human lives. Kovac and April promised vampire tenants a steady supply of blood under a contract stipulating they didn't kill the human guest. He reported offending vampires to the proper authorities when they'd killed an innocent in his hotel.

The female's scent in the room next to his beckoned him.

She smelled of vanilla and honeysuckle, two of his favorite scents. Her heart beat steadily, but not steadily enough to signal her slumber. Even if he gave into temptation to drink from her, he wouldn't enter her room until she slept.

He stuck with his routine, staring out the window at the people going about their business headed to or from Bourbon Street. It was mainly drunks on their way home or others just getting started for the night.

Startled by the sound of his adjoining door opening, Kovac turned around to see who entered his suite.

The most beautiful woman he'd ever seen stood in the doorway. His fingers itched to run through the thick, wavy, auburn hair that hung down her back and outlined her face. Her baby blue tank top pajama set with matching shorts brought out the blue in her sea-colored eyes, which tempted him to draw nearer. From what he could see, which was almost everything, his lips envied the freckles dusting nearly every inch of her milky skin.

With blood that still flowed through his body, the mere sight of her nearly caused an erection. Especially when he noticed her taut nipples poking through her barely-there top, begging to be sucked.

"May I come in?" the mysterious woman asked, bringing him out of his lust-filled stupor.

He hesitated. "Um, I guess so."

Living his second lifetime in New Orleans, the French Quarter held a spot in his soul as his favorite place to live. The tourism motto *Louisiana: Feed Your Soul* perfectly expressed the feeling this city buried inside of him all the way through to his bones.

Kovac had never brought a woman to the suite since moving back into the hotel a few years ago.

Women were easier to court when society regarded sex as sacred and not something everyone did with anybody they felt an attraction to.

He was old-fashioned, believing sex a sacred act. He'd given in to the idea of making love without a marriage license, but not to the concept of screwing any woman willing to let him. The women of this generation expected him to make love to them just because they batted their eyes in his direction. He still treasured the female species and didn't understand why women willingly gave up being treated as precious and valuable.

It was clear he had no plans to ask her why she opened his door.

"I'm sorry for barging in. Curiosity got the better of me. I was testing this skeleton key, thinking I must be letting my imagination run wild. I hoped to prove myself wrong—but here I am."

Kovac shrugged his shoulders and admitted, "You're the first to notice and try it, so we never bothered with updating the door locks. I guess we might have to look into it now that you've figured out our secret."

"Really?"

"Most people don't know what a skeleton key is, so they think nothing of it."

"But I'd assume your guests are historical fanatics who should have basic knowledge of keys."

He wanted to listen to her melodic voice forever. If love at first sight actually occurred, Kovac caught a severe case of it.

With the need to snap out of his feelings, he coldly answered, "We get thrill-seekers here, and not history buffs. This generation doesn't bother with facts. They're only looking for a good scare or a story to post on their Snapchat."

"So, how do I know you won't sneak into my room in the middle of the night and do things to me?" she teased him.

Ignoring the playful comment, to avoid encouraging her, he spoke the truth. "You don't know. You shouldn't worry, though. If I snuck into your room, you wouldn't remember I was ever there."

Chapter 6 ~ Nicole

Nicole's eyes grew enormous over his nonchalant attitude. His tone convinced her in such a way she worried he might actually sneak into her room.

She no longer felt comfortable talking with the handsome stranger, whoever he was. He must be a manager or the owner based on the way he answered her questions. He obviously wasn't a paying guest.

"Well, I won't bother you anymore," she told him while hastily making her way back into her room, where she pushed a chair up under the porcelain door handle. She then slid the dresser in front of the main door to her room.

It was only after rearranging the room that she realized it was futile. She dragged everything back into its proper place after having examined the eight-foot solid wooden doors—they opened out—not in. It was hopeless. If the ridiculously sexy man next door really wanted to come into her room, nothing in her power could deter him. She wasn't sure she even wanted to.

Ridiculously sexy didn't quite describe the ideas running through her head at first sight. His hair was mousy brown in a just-got-out-of-bed mess with stragglers hanging freely around his face. It drew her in. Her first instinct was a longing to brush the strands from his beautiful eyes to see them better combined with the need to get lost in them. She'd resisted the powerful urge that made her fingers twitch with desire.

His eyes reminded her of the woman who checked her into the hotel. They were so dark—they were almost black. Yet, they were drawing her to him. As if they were saying, "Come to me, my pretty," like a wicked witch in a fairy tale. The faint outline around his eyes only added to the come hither look he threw her way.

He had at least seven inches on top of her five-foot, eight-inch frame. His thinner build made her feel slightly less conscious of her frail physique. Even before the cancer, she struggled to put on pounds. It didn't matter what she ate, weight wouldn't stick to her bones. Last time she checked, she weighed a hundred and eleven pounds.

Nicole didn't know what actually possessed her to put the key in the lock of his door. She sat in the red armchair next to the rolltop desk in her room, holding the key. The key burned like fire in her grip, as though it was demanding to be used.

Back in her room, it looked even more horrific than the lobby. The dimly lit space only had wall sconces to light the room. She could barely see to read the brochure left on the desk.

Putting makeup on in the mornings would be impossible. Not that she wore makeup often. She believed a woman should be proud of her natural beauty instead of feeling the need to paint herself up. Women of this age looked more like drag queens and less like graceful beings created to showcase beauty. It was as if the female face was no longer something to be proud of but something to be embarrassed by.

One time in high school during a school project, the economics teacher tasked her and her class partner with making a budget. The girl wanted to set aside $300 a month for makeup.

Nicole shamefully let her thoughts vomit from her mouth. "If I was that ashamed of my face, I would just wear a paper bag." Needless to say, they never became best friends.

She moved her thoughts away from the lighting to take a moment of gratitude that at least the oak, four-poster, king-size bed with the white sheets and feather down duvet appeared fresh and clean.

There weren't any bugs slithering around, but her skin crawled, considering if all the lights were off, they might make an appearance.

Everything in the room appeared filthy with dust. It had to be part of the haunted vibe they were advertising and pulling off rather nicely.

At least housekeeping had cleaned the refrigerator and the microwave in the cabinet next to the dresser on the insides. Nicole would have drawn the line at food crumbs left behind to attract mice.

She moved the dust-coated, white, sheer curtains to reveal doors leading to a balcony overlooking the people walking up and down the streets. Stepping out onto her balcony, she encountered her gorgeous neighbor again.

Either he hadn't noticed her when she stepped outside, or he pretended not to. He appeared lost in thought as he stared across the street. His silhouette accented his thick, full lips. She momentarily longed to feel them on her skin. For some odd reason, she desperately wanted them on her neck, the one place she felt deathly ticklish.

Fear gripped her again, shaking her out of her hormone-induced fantasies. He could come into her room anytime he wanted to. She snuck back into the room, climbed into her bed, and tried to shake the man in the adjoining room out of her mind.

Chapter 7 ~ April

April passed her nights with various hobbies she'd taken up over the years. Usually, it was an arts and crafts project—tonight's choice of mind-numbing activity to pass the time was diamond painting.

The unexpected sound of a fire alarm startled her, causing her to knock all the tiny diamonds onto the carpet. She didn't bother to run to see what the commotion could be. The damn fire alarm was constantly going off. Assuming it was a false alarm, they'd taken to ignoring it. April crawled around on her hands and knees while cursing under her breath and was still picking up her diamonds when the firefighters showed up.

Guests from the third floor were coming down the stairs in a panic. It was the guest, Nicole, who told everyone what had them all in an uproar. "There is a man trying to bust the windows in the hallway open with a fire extinguisher."

Where could Kovac be? He'd gone up to his room a while ago and should have been able to stop the idiot.

The police and fire marshal commanded April to keep the guests calm while they handle everything else. The only thing she could think to calm the fools was to offer them a drink at the hotel bar. "The first one's on the house," she announced.

No one turned her down as she poured the handful of individuals a shot of their cheapest whiskey. She downed one herself since she had the bottle out, and to help with the headache nagging her from the fire alarm.

It took the police over twenty minutes to bring the individual down the stairs in handcuffs. The one in charge informed her that the man kept shouting about a monster in his room. He asked for the key to check it out to be on the safe side.

She gave him the key. Of course, whoever had snuck into the man's room would have long since gone. The terrified man told the truth; the terror-based stories were always the truth. It would be another story to add to the webpage to attract thrill seekers. They didn't intentionally create scares for guests, but when they happened, she and Kovac took advantage of them.

Most of the residents from the third floor were still pretty shaken up, and she had to pour them several more shots before they were ready to go back to sleep.

April impatiently wanted to check out the security footage, but first she trudged up the stairs to assess the damage.

With caution tape and a broom, she cleaned up the destruction. The moron busted through two of the three paneled glass windows on both ends of the hallway.

If he really wanted out of the building, he could have run down the stairs or jumped out of his balcony window. What possessed him to attempt an escape in such a brutal fashion? Besides the scare from the vampire who had snuck into his room, he must have been on something which wasn't unusual in their part of the city.

There was still no sign of Kovac when she sat down in the office to watch the security footage.

The terrified man was big, at least six and a half feet tall, thick, and burly. He ran from his room screaming, "Help! Help!" His cries for help went ignored.

At first, he tried to throw his body out the window, but he just bounced right off of the thick glass. With a running start, he tried the other window but once again failed.

Someone really should award her with a trophy or a plaque for keeping her mouth shut as much as she did, especially when there was so much that needed to be said about morons.

This dumbass then ripped the fire extinguisher box open with his bare hands and triggered the alarm, bringing the sleeping guests out of their rooms in the middle of the night.

He started on the north window, and when he didn't get it opened, he ran full force at the south window with the fire extinguisher.

The police tried to talk him down, but she couldn't hear what they said, as there was no sound. She only had her imagination to guess what the officers were telling him. Certainly, "Put down the fire extinguisher," came out of their mouths.

When talking him down proved futile, they fired their drawn tasers at the man. Four tasers were used to bring him to his knees before they could get close enough to cuff him. It took two pairs of handcuffs because of his size.

"Stupid fucking moron."

Chapter 8 ~ Kovac

Kovac jumped from his balcony to the street below, once the intoxicating woman next door to him went back inside of her room. A three-story jump should have caused attention, but passersby were too drunk to notice what should have been an impossible landing.

He noticed her immediately when she walked out of her door, yet he pretended not to. The temptation to win her heart already consumed him. She unknowingly had the power to compel him to her side. Facing her would put his emotions in a place he didn't want them to be.

The gorgeous redhead had burrowed herself under his skin in just the ten minutes in his presence, and he needed space before he did something he might regret.

On his walk through the Quarter, a sleezy brunette came on to him. He attempted to thwart her advances, and when she failed to take the hint, he backed her up into the closest alley to give her more than she begged for.

He pushed her roughly against a wall. Exactly the type of woman he despised. He missed the women who wanted to be pursued, who demanded romance, and who thought the marriage bed sacred.

Her attitude freed him of any guilt or shame he normally felt for what he was about to do. The woman took his aggression for desire when she eagerly pulled his lips to hers. The signals she put out told him she felt just fine with a bit of force. She practically screamed for more when he pushed her skirt up and drove his cold, calloused fingers inside of her.

Feeding came easier with the victim limber and satisfied. Plus, the euphoria from the venom in his fangs kept the human from crying out for help. After he emptied the female of nearly a pint of blood, he licked the wound closed with his saliva. He then released her. She slid to the ground from the weakened state she now found herself in.

Kovac walked away from her. Disgusted by her behavior and over his inconsolable need for human blood. He left her in a slump of confusion, mixed with satisfaction. He didn't look back because he never looked back at his victims.

Feeding was a necessary evil he couldn't avoid. The need for blood mimicked a heroin addict's need for their next fix. Only difference between him and a drug addict: at least a drug addict could get clean. There was no salvation from the pull of bloodlust in a vampire. His only choice was to pretend it didn't happen until next time. At least he could survive without for a couple days at a time before experiencing withdrawal. The older the vampire, the longer they could go without the need for blood.

Back at the hotel, he entered the office hearing April's everyday normal rant about humans. "Stupid fucking moron."

"What did I miss?"

April went through the ordeal, using more swear words than actual descriptive words, while replaying the surveillance footage for him.

Turning in the swivel office chair to look at him, she asked, "Where were you? You could have stopped the idiot before he did any damage."

"I went for a walk to clear my head."

"She got to you, too, didn't she?" April smirked.

He shoved his hands deep into the pocket of his jeans and admitted, "Maybe."

"She's probably sleeping by now if you want to pay her a visit," she teased, followed by a wink.

"I already fed tonight, and I have no intention of drinking from her." Kovac's voice was laced with defiance.

"That bad, huh? I told you, you would like her."

"It doesn't matter. You know I won't do anything about it."

"One of these days, I might just do it for you," she threatened.

"You wouldn't dare."

April stood up to face her friend, nearly a foot shorter than him. She had to strain her head to look into his eyes. With a defiant tone, she challenged Kovac, "Try me."

It was the same argument they had been having for three centuries. He threw his hands up in the air and backed out of the room.

His last words to his well-intentioned friend before heading back to his room: "I mean it, April, don't you dare."

The sun would be up shortly, and the burning in his eyes from the stress of his neighbor had him desperately longing to close his lids. Maybe he would sleep the desire for her off. And people in hell want ice water.

Chapter 9 ~ Nicole

Nicole woke after an hour with a splitting headache caused by the tumor in her brain. She tossed and turned, but didn't find any proper rest until the sun came up. She slept through most of the day.

After a shower, she headed downstairs to the lobby for recommendations on a place to find a meal. Maybe food would ease her headache. She had eaten nothing since arriving in New Orleans, and for once her stomach growled in protest. Her appetite had been waning and non-existent lately.

The same woman who checked her in sat behind the front desk, still wearing the same pink wig. Today's t-shirt was simple: it read, *Ew, people.*

The man from the adjoining room next to hers stood beside her as they looked at something on the computer.

It didn't seem possible, but he looked even sexier today than he did yesterday. She had settled on the notion she would die a virgin, but he had her contemplating checking off losing her virginity from her bucket list.

She had opportunities to have sex with her handful of boyfriends, but they lacked the ability to make her weak enough in the knees to say yes. She regretted her picky attitude after the doctors she had consulted diagnosed her.

Nicole patiently waited while the pair discussed business. The young woman noticed her first and asked, "Can we help you with something?"

"Um, I wondered if you could recommend a place to eat. Somewhere within walking distance, please." Her words stumbled out of her mouth because his presence made her nervous.

"Our favorite place is about a twenty-minute walk. Kovac could show you where it is." The female boldly offered her friend's assistance.

Neither Nicole nor Kovac responded to the suggestion. They both awkwardly stared at one another, waiting to see who might say something first. Kovac's friend elbowed him when the silence continued unbroken.

He composed himself to say, "Yes, absolutely. It's not safe for a young lady like yourself to walk these streets alone after dark. I'd be happy to accompany you."

Unsure of why she agreed to his help without hesitation, Nicole told Kovac, "If it's not too much trouble, thank you."

She couldn't take her eyes off him as he walked around the counter toward her in his tight jeans and plain white t-shirt, which he'd tucked into his belt at the center, letting the rest hang free over his jeans. She'd sucked her lip in with her teeth, daydreaming about pulling his shirt out of the belt and over his head to see the muscles in his abs.

Walking to the front door, she caught a view of his full shaped bottom. She hadn't moved while checking him out. "Are you coming?" he asked her as he held the door open for her.

Quickly, she caught up to him, but not without awkwardly

tripping over her feet on the way. She then stepped out the door onto the streets of the French Quarter. The hotel entrance sat on a side street next to Bourbon Street.

Kovac began walking toward Bourbon Street. without saying a word. She kept pace beside his long legs.

He'd positioned himself to walk along the buildings while she walked on the street side. Most gentlemen kept to the street side when escorting a lady, but she imagined he placed her on the street side to keep her safe from whatever or whoever might lurk along the buildings and alleys.

They continued their journey in silence. Nicole's emotions were too much all over the place to start a conversation with the man whose sensual yet scary presence made it hard for her to breathe steadily. Unsure of what his thoughts might be about the other woman volunteering his services. She worried he felt put out for having to chaperone her through the city.

After turning onto Canal Street, Nicole tried to pay attention to her surroundings; she didn't want to depend on his help in the future. Her eye caught a few shops she wouldn't mind window-shopping in. Not that she planned to buy souvenirs she couldn't take with her to the afterlife. She also noted other places she might find a good meal.

They turned off Canal Street onto South Peters Street—still, two strangers refusing to speak to one another. Nicole felt equally terrified and attracted to Kovac.

When they turned on to Julia Street, Kovac informed her, "It's not much further. Less than half a mile on this street."

His voice sounded thick and deep, as if he came from a distant land, hiding his true voice. It only added to his sex appeal. Her emotions played her like a piano out of tune. While the darkness she saw in him scared her, if he asked her to join him in his bed, she wouldn't hesitate to say yes.

Taking several deep breaths, Nicole worked up the courage to ask him, "Where are we going?"

"Mulate's," he shortly replied.

As the restaurant came into view, the two-story building gave her pause. It sat at the intersection of two streets. Julia Street was on the east and Convention Center Boulevard was on the north, making the door placement on neither street but at the exact point where the streets intersect, putting it directly in the center of the structure. What made it different from the usual construction of a building, instead of designing a corner on the restaurant, the wall had been cut off at a forty-five-degree angle, therefore eliminating the ninety-degree corner now creating two forty-five-degree walls with a door right in the center.

A covered porch type walkway hung low underneath the second story, which looked unused. Pillars set every couple of feet braced the roof of the cover.

The large trifold sign read *Mulate's* painted in the center of the building. It hung directly above the entrance, giving it a winged look on both side streets. Whichever direction one came from, they could easily find the restaurant with the three different signs. Above the center sign read *World Famous* and underneath *The Original Cajun Restaurant.* The letters were all printed in a shade of red.

Kovac acted the faithful gentleman and pulled open the baby blue-green wooden door for her. She walked in to hear the sounds of Cajun music. She turned her head in the direction of the music playing. A stage sat at the back of the restaurant with a live band playing the sounds of New Orleans.

Her assistant must've been a regular, as the hostess called him by name and asked him if he wanted his usual table. The hostess escorted them to a table in the darkest corner of the room.

When they were seated with menus in hand, she told him, "My name is Nicole Ripp, by the way."

He stared hard at the menu, avoiding looking up at her, as he responded, "I go by Kovac Nikoli."

What an odd way to introduce oneself. And did she hear a hint of a Russian accent in the way he said his name?

She couldn't help herself when she asked him, "You go by Kovac. What does that even mean? Is Kovac your name or isn't it?"

"It's the name I chose for myself more than a thousand years ago when I left my birth name behind."

Nicole stared at him in confusion. Surely, he must jest. Before she could ask, their server came over to take their drink orders.

"My usual, vodka straight," he told her.

"A glass of Moscato, please," Nicole ordered.

"Any particular brand?" the server asked.

"Anything is fine. You pick."

The server left the two sitting awkwardly at the table to begin their conversation again. Before Nicole could ask about his thousand years' comment, Kovac asked, "Why are you in New Orleans?"

For some unexplainable reason, something compelled her to tell him the truth. "I'm looking for a place to spend my last days, and New Orleans called my soul."

Kovac finally looked up from his menu he had been staring at silently. Which he clearly had not been reading it because it was upside down. "Your last days?"

"Yes, I have an inoperable tumor in my brain. I plan to spend what days I have left making the most of them."

"You're not actually serious, are you?" he asked, perplexed.

"I'm more serious than you were with your thousand years' comment," she pointedly told him.

He rushed through, ignoring her comment about his thousand years to ask her, "How much longer do you have?"

"They couldn't give me an exact time. The doctors said when the end gets near, I'd be able to tell because I'll start to lose my normal body functions, my headaches will get worse, and I'll probably start having seizures. I may even go blind."

Nicole told him everything. It seemed like an unknown force beckoned it out of her.

Before they could continue the conversation, the server came to the table with their drinks. She asked Kovac, "Do you want me to put in your usual order?"

With his eyes still searching Nicole, he told the girl, "Give us a few minutes."

The wave of discomfort his questioning eyes caused forced her to change the subject. "What do you usually order?"

"I always order the appetizer for two. It comes with a bit of everything you can imagine that one would enjoy about Cajun cuisine. April and I usually split it."

"That sounds good. We can order that. I'll split it with you if you want to," she said, not bothering to look at the menu.

"So, who is April?" she asked with a tinge of jealousy in her voice.

A hint of a smirk appeared on his face, revealing he recognized she might feel jealous. "April is my sister, my best friend and business partner. She's the girl working the counter who suggested we go out tonight."

She blushed at the knowing grin. "Oh," she said, feeling relieved, which she failed to hide from her voice, causing the redness in her cheeks to deepen.

Chapter 10 ~ Kovac

Kovac told her the truth about his name and his age. Something about her drew it out of him. She probably wouldn't believe him, but he still said it, uncertain why he didn't want to lie to her. Even though his and April's lie that they were siblings flowed out of his mouth out of habit, everything else was the truth. He felt tempted to correct that lie, but refrained.

When she told him she was dying, the unexplainable pain in his soul over the idea that this beautiful creature would cease to exist before long was an ache he'd never experienced. Worse than any time he'd walked away from someone he believed he loved.

After several minutes of awkward silence, she made the comment, "If only there was a God who didn't let things like this happen to people like me."

"You don't believe in God?" he curiously asked.

"No, why would I? A good God wouldn't let bad things like this happen to good people." Her voice was laced with bitterness. Her emotions were clear in every sentence she spoke.

"I disagree," he admitted to her before continuing, "If He stepped in and changed everything in this world after the fall of man, He would have to take away our free will. And that's the most important thing He gave humanity. He gave us free will to do the things we've done to this world and the things we've done to our bodies. Otherwise, we would just be robots."

"Are you saying it's my fault, and that I did this to my body?" she asked defensively, just shy of angry.

He already loved how she wore every feeling on her sleeve for him to see. "No, not at all. I'm saying that throughout history, humans have violated the planet, the atmosphere, our food, and everything else you can think of. The fact that our bodies are riddled with diseases that we can't control is because of what we've done to nature. Sadly, we pay the price of what past generations have done on this earth. Like I said, He would've had to stop their free will to keep things from affecting us the way they do."

"You're a believer in God, then? You and Him are friends?" Sadness seeped from her tone.

"No, I turned my back on Him a long time ago. We're definitely not friends, but I know He exists."

The debate came to a close with the arrival of their meal. Kovac had ordered the appetizer platter or, as Mulate's called it, *Grande Plateau de Hors d'oeuvres*, which came with grilled alligator bites and frog legs, fried calamari, tilapia bites and popcorn shrimp, stuffed mushrooms, meat pies, and their Cajun boudin. The dish was supposed to feed four to six people according to the menu description, but Kovac never had a problem finishing it with April's help.

Nicole's mesmerizing, ocean-colored eyes, which were grayer tonight, had grown into giant saucers over the size of the platter. He loved the color of her eyes, and found himself sad that if she found out about vampires and asked for the change, that she would lose the color of her sexy eyes. There wasn't any rhyme or reason for it, but all vampires' eyes turned a deep brown, almost black, after becoming immortal. As if it was evidence in the windows of their souls, someone had drained them of their mortal lives.

After her initial shock, she told him, "You weren't kidding when you said it comes with a bit of everything."

"And you—" Kovac picked up a plate "—must try at least one piece of everything." He took his fork and filled a plate before handing it to her.

His hand brushed against hers when she reached for the plate. Their eyes met, causing Kovac's heart to melt with desire for this beautiful woman. Not just a sexual desire, but one of longing to know all there was to know about her with her gorgeous, auburn hair spread out across his pillow as a bonus.

She'd most likely be very willing to choose immortality on earth over death. It never occurred to him to search for an eternal companion amongst the dying. Still, could he curse her with this existence that offered no reprieve from the woes of this world?

If and when April found out, she wouldn't hesitate to offer Nicole the choice. And there would be nothing he could say or do to stop his friend.

Kovac hadn't even taken a bite of his food as he watched Nicole take her first bite. With each nibble a silent moan escaped her lips, causing a desire to rise in him. He imagined her making those same noises as she lay beneath him, breathless and satisfied. He needed a distraction because he did not want to think about her that way. Not right now.

"What about your family? What about your friends?"

She looked up at him with a look of guilt. "I left them a note without saying goodbye. I figured it's easier this way. They don't have to watch me die. I'm going to die, anyway. They would have had to say goodbye to me at some point. Death is always unexpected. I just made it come quicker for them. I wouldn't be surprised if there were missing posters up everywhere with my face on it, though."

What could he say to her confession? Was there a correct response? He'd done the same thing over a thousand years ago. He left his family without a goodbye, except he didn't leave a note. At least she left a note.

"Am I a terrible person?" A tear fell from her eye with the sadness in her question.

"I don't think so. You did what you felt in your heart to do. No one should fault you for that. Besides, they do not know what you're going through. I can't imagine how scared you are."

"I'm terrified," she admitted.

Thinking about her lying beneath him might have been an easier subject. The idea of her frayed and dying, knowing he could help her, wrenched his gut. Not knowing if it was the right thing to do felt equally painful.

Instead of offering words of comfort or changing the subject or saying anything else at all, he reached out and grabbed her hand. She seemed to welcome his hand when she squeezed it in return.

"Would you like to dance? Maybe take your mind off of things for a while?"

Nicole eagerly accepted his suggestion.

Fortunately, they played a slow song because Kovac would have been lost if it had been a Cajun two step. He had never taken the time to learn any dance moves in his long life.

He pulled her in close against his body. She felt like home. Her slender body fit perfectly against his thin frame. Having her so close, her intoxicating scent was nearly irresistible. His fangs punched through his gums in anticipation of what she would taste like. He forced them back in because she was the last person he would ever drink from just to quench his thirst.

Chapter 11 ~ April

April could hear a guest stomping down the stairs of the hotel and through the lobby with her heightened hearing. Already sensing it was a human, frustrated and looking to complain about something, she braced herself to prepare for the moron.

The gentleman leaned over the counter, banging on the call bell while shouting, "Is anyone here that can helppp me?" He emphasized the p, as if it'd bring her to his aid more quickly.

By the time she forced herself to make an appearance, his anger level had increased. He waved around a rather large-size dildo in her face. "I found this in the chair in my room," he loudly told her.

The idiot flopped it around like a wet noodle. He didn't even bother to wrap it in a towel or put it in a laundry bag. Nope, he had the device in his hand. No telling if anyone had cleaned it. And why would they have?

"Well, I'm not touching it," April told the man.

"It's absolutely disgusting. Housekeeping should have found it and taken care of it. If they missed this, what else did they miss? Did they even clean my room?" Clearly uncomfortable over the situation, yet he still waved it around for all to see.

"If it's so disgusting—" April extended a trash can for him to throw it into "—why are you carrying it around so proudly?"

She'd pissed him off with her question, but he had it coming. *He's really a fucking moron.* She kept the words in her head she desperately wanted to say. She even wished she had worn her other t-shirt that read, *Sometimes I look at you and wonder why no one has thrown a brick at you yet.*

Before being forced to contend further with the ridiculous human, the fire alarm activated. The pitch blared annoyingly. Having super hearing, as a vampire, anytime the alarm went off, a major headache was guaranteed to follow if not dealt with quickly, like the one she suffered through last night because of the incessant noise.

The disgruntled moron still leaned against the counter like she could make his stay somehow magically more memorable than finding a used sex toy in his room. Hoping he would get the hint that she would do nothing to compensate him, she went in search of what caused the offensive noise. She used the fire alarm as an excuse to walk away from the conversation she knew could go on for several more minutes.

April should have waited for the fire department like she did last night. Anything to get away from the fool at the front desk, though. And she could handle herself, no matter the problem.

She started on the third floor. Not seeing anything out of the ordinary, she moved on to the second floor and then the first. At the very last room at the end of the hall, she noticed water pouring from under the door. At the same time, the fire department rounded the corner to meet up with her.

April moved out of the way to let the hunky firemen

bang on the door. April forgot about the noise momentarily. She couldn't take her eyes off one of the humans in his uniform. She had no intention of finding a happily ever after like Kovac, but that never stopped her from a good lay.

The annoyingly sexy man snapped his fingers in her face to get her attention. "There is no answer. Can you open the door?"

Shaking herself out of her hormonal stupor, she answered him, "Oh, yes." Pulling a key from her pocket, she unlocked the door and walked into the room.

April and the firefighters stood in almost an inch of water, while getting equally soaked with the water spraying down from the ceiling.

Hanging from the ceiling was a hammock chair, along with the water sprinkler. The chair appeared to have been hooked to the sprinkler. The dumb humans who thought hanging something from a sprinkler a bright idea were nowhere to be seen.

"Stupid fucking morons," April mumbled under her breath. She walked away, telling the men, "I can't deal with this shit."

After changing her clothes, she stopped at the bar and poured herself a double shot of Gentleman Jack.

By the time she calmed her anger over another guest's stupid activity, she put her big girl panties on to clean up the mess. She carried to the room a shop vac, towels, and a mop. The firemen had stopped the water and alarm, and were picking up their equipment when she walked into the room.

She slipped a note to one of the men, the one who'd given her a reason for needing another fresh pair of panties. Sweat dripped from his handsome brow. His masculine scent nearly brought out her fangs in anticipation of his blood slipping down her throat.

The note just had her room number on it. Surely, he had enough intelligence to understand her meaning, because a romantic note was not in her skill set. And if he couldn't figure out her meaning, his stupidity alone would put out the fire in between her thighs, revoking his invitation.

Chapter 12 ~ Nicole

After one dance, they headed back to the table to eat their food. The food was some of the best food she had ever put in her mouth.

Kovac even seemed less scary the more she talked to him. His eyes were pools of dark, mysterious danger, but she wanted to stare into them and learn all of his secrets. Even the evil ones he surely carried.

Maybe it was her desire for him to tell her things he had never told a soul that kept her spilling all of her problems. As a twenty-four-year-old, dying virgin who ran away from everyone she loved and hated, she carried a lot of baggage.

He still never answered her question about his thousand-year comment, and her curiosity got the better of her. The longer they talked, the more inclined she was to believe he wasn't joking.

They had finished their entire platter, and she was on the verge of asking him about his age when the owner or manager interrupted them.

As a regular, Kovac seemed pretty popular. The owner was a beautiful Creole woman, he introduced as Shantell. The sparkle in her big, brown eyes betrayed her attraction to Kovac, who appeared to be either oblivious to it or just not interested.

He acted cordial while she flirted, despite Nicole sitting at the table with him. A possessive feeling stirred in her gut, making her antsy. Her body gave away her emotions as she uncomfortably swayed side to side in her seat. She tried to ignore her irrational feelings until Shantell stroked Kovac's arm. She stifled the growl that attempted to escape her mouth without permission. A deep-seated feeling that he belonged to her and no one else ran through her core. They just met. How could he belong to her? And don't forget the grim reaper coming for her any day.

Before her fist could get any bright ideas, Nicole stood up, reached her hand out, and asked Kovac, "Will you teach me how to dance to this music?"

The sexiest smile she had ever seen beamed across his face. Her attempt to rescue him from the unwanted attention was obvious. It wasn't dimples that formed when he broke out into the first smile he'd graced her with. The only way to describe it was three deep lines that traveled from just under each eye, all the way down to his chin. He looked beautiful when he smiled and should do it more often.

Kovac willingly granted her request. He stood up and politely excused himself. Did he ever do anything ungentlemanly? "Thank you for your hospitality, Shantell. As always, everything was splendid." He reached for Nicole's extended hand and gracefully escorted her to the dance floor.

On the floor, he pulled Nicole into his arms to whisper into her ear, "I don't know how to dance to this music, but thank you for the distraction."

She threw her head back and laughed at his confession. All her anguish was quenched by being in his arms. "Well, I usually pick things up pretty easily. It seems fairly simple. Just watch and do what everyone else is doing," she encouraged him.

It didn't take long for the couple to figure out the rhythm of the dance steps. Moving their feet together back and forth and side to side in a two-step. He even elegantly spun her around, along with the other dancers, before she nearly collapsed in his arms from exhaustion. The cancer that was her death sentence wore her out quicker than the average healthy person.

He grabbed her around her waist to hold her up. She didn't want him to let her go, and he didn't seem to be in any hurry to do so either. A slow song played as if the band knew neither wanted to stop dancing but needed a less strenuous dance.

Nicole wrapped her arms up around his neck. She wanted to be the reason the smile on his face hadn't waned since they stepped onto the floor. Resisting the urge no longer, she brushed the loose strands of hair from his eyes, and told him, "You should always smile."

Chapter 13 ~ Kovac

Kovac repeatedly thought about kissing her perfect lips since she asked him to teach her to dance. *It's too soon. This is not a date.* There were many reasons not to kiss her. When Nicole moved the hair from his eyes, his lips forgot all the reasons he formulated and took over to claim hers. Animalistic instincts screamed *Mine* from deep inside of him.

Vampires did not have soulmates or destined other halves. The lucky ones fell in love, but quickly found out, after decades or centuries with an eternal partner, that love is not always a feeling. Loving someone forever starts out as a feeling, but choosing a life partner means you choose to love them, even when those feelings change. If you can fall in love, then you can fall out of love. Choosing to love someone has more power and lasts longer rather than falling for someone.

As Nicole parted her lips in invitation, Kovac accepted her invite. His tongue searched the crevices of her mouth, while her tongue mimicked his movements.

Having fallen in and out of love many times in his millennia, kissing Nicole, he felt his heart choosing her. He grasped the trouble he found himself in, and his conscience already warred within him. But he didn't care, as he held her in his arms.

It took the music ending for him to let go of the first woman who had his conscience shouting, "Morals be damned."

His loins, his heart, and his mind were screaming to carry her home to offer her immortality. He could not bear the idea of a world without Nicole in it, and he barely knew her. His soul whispered slightly louder when he said, "I apologize for being so forward. I don't know what came over me."

Nicole's eyes studied his, as if she looked to discover something deep within him. Having her wrapped in his arms and pressed up against his chest, releasing her became the last thing on his mind. Nicole didn't appear to want to escape his embrace, either.

"You should never say you're sorry unless you actually mean it," she teased before chewing on her bottom lip.

Kovac laughed at her remark. It was something he rarely did. Joy was an emotion he left behind a long time ago.

"I'll rephrase. I'm not sorry for kissing you. I am sorry for not asking permission first."

"Asking permission destroys the magic of a first kiss," she unashamedly confessed. The desire for him seeping from the glint in her eyes added to his dilemma.

April always sat like a mini devil on his shoulder telling him to make a mate. Kovac sat like a tiny angel on his other shoulder, reminding him of the moral repercussions. The mini devil had a new friend sitting next to her on his shoulder and her name was Nicole Ripp.

The crowded restaurant probably stared at the couple standing on the dance floor in each other's arms while the band packed up for the night. Neither cared what anyone thought, as they were both mesmerized by each other.

The two would have stayed the way they were for hours, but Shantell interrupted them to tell them the restaurant needed to close.

Kovac let go of Nicole grudgingly to pay the bill. Once outside, she boldly reached for his hand, laced her fingers through his, and snuggled up close to him, where she belonged, for the walk back to the hotel.

They strolled back in silence. Kovac wanted to learn all there was to know about the beautiful redhead who captured every piece of him. He held back, terrified that by discovering all about who she was, he would not be able to let her just die without a choice.

Why Nicole walked quietly added mystery to their time, but it was not one Kovac sought to solve. He knew peace most likely waited for her on the other side of death, and all he wanted to do was selfishly offer her a cursed life on this side with him for all eternity.

He thought about April and what she would say about his predicament. "We live in an age where people's morals adapt to whatever their circumstances are, so screw—" (she would have used the other word) "—your conscience and do what you want to better yourself."

Stepping through the doors of his hotel, he spotted April shooting back shots of whiskey at the bar. She had on a fresh shirt since he left with Nicole for dinner. This one read *I don't like to think before I speak. I like to just be as surprised as everyone else about what comes out of my mouth.*

"Rough night?" Nicole asked her before he could.

"Just take a walk and look in room 103. You have to see it to believe it," April told them, offering no further clues about her night.

Still holding hands, Kovac led Nicole to room 103. April had carried a mop and a bucket into the room, but clearly said, "Screw—" (again, she would have used the other word) "—this shit," and walked away from the mess.

"Oh my," Nicole said with her hand over her mouth in an attempt to stifle her laughter.

Kovac joined her in laughing, causing her to release what she had been trying to hold back out of politeness.

Some idiot thought it a good idea to hang a chair hammock from the water sprinkler. April was right. More often than not, people were stupid.

The wooden floors had buckled from the water that lingered on the surface from having not been dried up.

The residents of the room left their belongings behind and appeared to have climbed out the window they left hanging open. Too cowardly to face the consequences of their actions.

"Maybe we should join April for a drink," Kovac suggested.

"You sure? I don't mind helping clean up." Nicole suggested.

"Nah, that's what we pay our staff for. Management can handle it when they come in."

Chapter 14 ~ April

April threw back her sixth whiskey shot of the night and watched Kovac walk down the hall, holding the human girl's hand. That shot was a celebratory shot, instead of a stress one like all the others.

Stress could be her middle name. It was the excuse Kovac gave everyone who came to the desk complaining about her. "She's just stressed," he always told them. Not having a more polite explanation for her attitude. She'd be richer than she already was if she had a nickel for every time someone threatened to have her fired. Any stress she felt this night lifted upon seeing the loving look in Nicole's eyes for Kovac.

She set the shot glass down on the bar when her fireman walked through the front doors. Pouring herself another shot and one for the tall drink of blood that approached her. Her third pair of panties of the night quickly soaked, certain the fireman's intention was to take her up on the invitation she'd slipped into his pocket earlier.

He sat down at the bar and asked her, "What's your name, beautiful?"

"Is my name really important? You didn't walk in that

door to get to know me, did you?"

"Fair enough. When do you get off?" His tantalizing voice matched the sex appeal his entire vibe put out. He was hot, and he seemed to know it. The black t-shirt he wore pulled against his taunt pectoral muscles. She couldn't wait to get her fill of them in her hands.

April poured him another drink. He didn't hesitate to throw it back. She admired the muscles in his neck as the warm liquid slid down his throat.

Kovac came back with Nicole after checking out the fiasco in room 103, so she asked him, "Can you finish my shift for me?"

She didn't wait for his response as she walked away with her fireman following. It was more of a statement than a request, anyway. The friends rarely turned the other down when they wanted off for whatever reason.

In her room, her fireman lifted his shirt over his head the second she closed the door. His chest looked even more sexy than she'd imagined. The veins pulsing in his neck were clearly visible.

April didn't care about foreplay, which involved tenderness and emotions. She just wanted a good fuck, and this stranger, with his rugged good looks, certainly would give her what she wanted.

When she stripped out of her clothes, he took the hint and removed the rest of his. He held his length in the grip of his hand while he backed up against the edge of her bed. It symbolized the unspoken question: "What do you want me to do now?"

In answer to his question, she shoved him down onto the bed before climbing on top of him. She took control for the moment, and he didn't offer up any objections when she brought her core down on his shaft.

He lasted longer than most, allowing her to climax twice before he flipped her over. Neither had initiated a kiss until he had her on her back, which was fine with her. She allowed him to kiss her only because he gave as good as she did.

Once he climaxed, he laid across her body, spent, giving her easy access to his neck. Her fangs lengthened before she plunged them into his throbbing vein. She had worn him out enough that he had no fight left in him as she pulled the blood from him.

Careful not to take too much from him, she licked the puncture closed with her healing venom and shoved him off her when she finished. He had passed out while she drank his blood, like most of her partners did. Men were weak after sex. Add losing a pint of blood, and they were putty.

Leaving him to sleep it off for a bit, April made her way to the shower.

Once dressed in one of her signature t-shirts and a pair of gym shorts, she lit up one of her clove cigarettes while she sat on her balcony watching the sunrise.

The sun didn't set vampires on fire like the myths would have you believe. It only affected them as if they were severely allergic to sunlight, which caused severe burns and blisters. It's possible if a vampire attempted to spend any length of time in the sun, their skin might fall off. As far as April knew, the severity of the burns and blisters kept any sane vampire from standing in the sun long enough to test the hypothesis.

A cigarette and a sunrise happened to be two of the few moments in life that brought her temporary peace. She took every opportunity to watch the sunrise. When the beautiful sun stood high enough in the sky to cause her pain, she went back to her room to find her fireman had woken up and left.

She crawled under her covers to sleep the day away,

thankful he left before she had to drag him out of her bed. April didn't share her bed with anyone.

Chapter 15 ~ Nicole

Having stayed up with Kovac till after sunrise, Nicole again slept the day away. His face, his hands, his lips, his touch, and more filled her dreams. So much that getting out of bed felt tortuous.

She'd sat with him for the rest of the night after April left him to man the hotel. Sitting with Kovac while he worked, she understood why April thought people were idiots.

One person called with a question and actually asked if they should bring their own sheets? When has a hotel ever not provided sheets?

A call from a guest's room asking for help to use the phone made her laugh 'till she couldn't breathe. Seriously, he was using the phone he claimed he couldn't get to work. Kovac, the forever gentlemen, surprised her when he asked the individual, "Don't you have a cell phone you could use?" He must have had an inner April hidden deep within that slipped out occasionally.

Another couple came to the front desk asking for a drink tray, like the hotel was a fast-food restaurant.

In between helping his paying patrons, they talked until his relief arrived in the morning. If Nicole had been like every other woman on the planet, they might have talked about her hopes and dreams. She no longer had any of those.

Reliving her past had become too difficult to talk about. She had already put it all behind her, so why dredge it up?

He gave her the impression that he wanted to open himself up to her, but something held him back.

Kovac walked her to her door, where he leaned in to gently slide his lips along hers. His words still echoed in her ears, "Sleep well, my beautiful Nicole." He called her his, and she wasn't quite sure what to make of that.

She loved the idea of being his, but that wouldn't be fair to him. He deserved someone to share his life with, not someone who could go to sleep at any time and never wake up.

Then again, he knew she was dying. Her insecurities kicked in, telling her maybe he didn't want a commitment and thought her perfect for the temporary relationship he preferred.

Nicole slept in spurts. Her dreams filled with Kovac woke her several times. The sun had already begun to set when she dragged herself out of the bed.

By the time she had showered and put herself together, she'd talked herself into believing the worst of Kovac. Still wanting her fears to be lies, maybe she could find April to see if his sister could shed some light on his motives.

If she knew which room belonged to April, she would have started there, knowing Kovac worked the desk tonight.

Nicole roamed the hotel, avoiding the front desk as she searched for April.

Her quest brought her to a set of antique French doors that swung open onto the brick back patio. Inside, the hotel looked nearly in shambles and appeared neglected in so many ways. The setting outside almost took her breath away.

It seemed as if she had stepped into a real-life version of *The Secret Garden*. Her low-heeled shoes clacked against the narrow brick walkway. It wasn't the yellow brick road, but it might as well have been as she followed its path along the thick wild gardens.

Wildflowers grew on every side of the path. The gardens were filled to overflowing with every color imaginable, yet it was devoid of any weeds. This garden looked well-tended and loved by someone.

Turning around to check her path, worried she might get lost, she discovered ivy vines crawling up the back of the hotel. Only small sections of the brick building could be seen behind the wall of vines.

Her heart beat faster, thinking she might not find her way back. But the pull to keep going felt stronger. The wildflowers were endless, but further along the path, various types of trees and bushes grew amidst the gardens. She recognized crepe myrtles, holly trees, and rose bushes, but nothing else she found familiar.

After several twists and turns, the brick path led her to a center courtyard of what she imagined was the most beautiful and cared for garden in the city. The focal point of the garden was an old sugar kettle, probably a find from a local sugar plantation. Wrought-iron tables outlined the massive cast-iron kettle directly in the middle of the garden, where April sat in one of the matching chairs.

Even more magnificent than the garden were the many birds surrounding April. Birds of blue, of red, of green, and even multicolored birds walked along the bricks, eating the bird seed scattered along the ground.

Nicole's mouth dropped when a gorgeous brown owl splattered with white spots landed on April's shoulder. An unbelievable feat, considering owls have sharp talons.

"Are you going to keep staring, or are you going to join me?" April asked her.

It startled Nicole that April knew she was behind her. She couldn't remember making any noise as she approached.

Lost in awe of her surroundings, the question, "What is... is this place?" stumbled from her mouth.

"This is my little piece of heaven on earth."

Nicole walked closer to the table, startling the owl, causing him to fly up into a tree.

"Come sit with me," April encouraged Nicole.

Nicole's eyes landed on April's choice of shirt for the day. *Alright, I'm up. Let's spread the fuckery.* She tried to hide her laugh but failed.

"You like my shirt?"

Nicole nodded and said, "How many shirts like that do you own?"

"Who knows? I have a Cricut machine, so I make a couple of new ones every week. I'm actually thinking about putting them in a book. I'd call it *How to Tell Idiots to Shut the Fuck Up.*" April's attitude probably offended most, but Nicole respected her unrestrained point of view.

April definitely wore wigs, because today's choice, a teal blue bob, framed her face nicely. "What do you think of Kovac?" she asked Nicole while lighting up a black cigarette.

Being on death's door, Nicole spoke frank and straight from the heart. "I've never met anyone who makes me feel the way he does."

There gleamed a hint of delight mingled with mischief

behind April's dark eyes. Nicole waited to see if April would offer any insight on what kind of man he was. After several drags and nothing, she boldly asked, "Is he the kind of man that only wants a temporary relationship?"

"There is only one thing in this world he has sought but never found, and that is someone to spend forever with. What makes you think he is only looking for a fling?"

Nicole didn't hesitate when she confessed, "I told him I have a terminal illness, and that didn't scare him away. He actually seemed like it didn't bother him. When he said goodnight to me, he called me his beautiful Nicole. Why would he call me his when he knows I can't give him a happily ever after, unless he is the kind of man who enjoys a casual, temporary relationship?"

"What I would consider a weakness if it were me is Kovac's greatest quality. He only knows how to love and how to commit."

April's words shook Nicole to the core. She stood up and walked back to the hotel, lost in her own thoughts and a bit in shock. She didn't even say thank you or goodbye to April.

Chapter 16 ~ Kovac

Kovac expected Nicole would have joined him at the start of his shift. Disappointment crept in when she didn't show up right away. Certain she felt drawn to him the way he did to her. After a couple of hours of waiting in vain, he thought maybe his certainty was nothing more than wishful thinking.

Lying in bed after the sun came up, he went back and forth with himself on whether he should offer Nicole immortality. As many times as he had loved before, his heart never ached at the thought of their death. He actually never considered a world without the women whom he spent time with.

He justified offering to turn her, because surely if he told her the horrible truths surrounding eternal life in this body, she would choose death. Would he have chosen this path had he known completely what he was getting himself into?

If she didn't feel for him as strongly as he did for her already, then all his tortuous thoughts over turning her were a moot point.

The sound of her heartbeat, music to his ears, reverberated in his ear drums before she came into view. Just like fingerprints, a person's heartbeat is unique. He studied her heartbeat last night, as it called his name. In a sea of people, he would be able to find her by the rhythm of her heart.

The closer she got to him, her scent of vanilla and honeysuckle engulfed him. The smile that had formed on his face quickly disappeared when she rounded the corner. She appeared distressed.

Kovac jumped over the counter in haste, desperate to ease whatever caused her obvious pain.

"What's the matter, my beautiful Nicole?"

She looked up at him, dead in the eyes. "I'm dying. There is no changing that. So how can you claim me as yours?"

Kovac nervously ran his hand through his messy hair that stopped right at his collar, unsure how to answer her question.

"Well?" she asked. She then walked over to the counter, leaned her slender frame against it, crossed her arms, and began tapping her foot, waiting for him to respond.

Moving to stand in front of her where she stood, he placed his hands on the counter, trapping her in place. He looked into her eyes to admit to her, "Whether we have one day together, one month together, or an eternity, my heart claimed you from the moment I laid eyes on you."

"This won't change my mind to have the surgery, or chemotherapy, just to add a few months to my life."

"I know, and I wouldn't ask you to, because I respect and understand your feelings about that."

She appeared to be studying him, trying to figure out if he meant what he said.

"My heart claimed you, too," she admitted before reaching up on her toes to kiss the lips she wished she could carry with her into the afterlife.

Kovac didn't resist as he wrapped his arms around her waist to lift her tiny frame into his arms up off the ground to carry her into his office, where they would have more privacy.

Having just set her back down on her feet, he nearly growled when the bell at the front desk forced him to let go of her completely.

With one more peck on her perfect lips, he told her, "I'll try not to be long. Will you wait here for me?"

She nodded at him while he seared a memory in his mind of her desire for him shining forth from her gorgeous, blue-green eyes, which were greener because of the blouse she wore, patterned white with subtle green vertical stripes.

At the hotel counter, Kovac acted on his best behavior despite the frustration he felt from being interrupted. "I am sorry to keep you waiting. How may I help you?" he asked the man standing before him.

"I am looking for a friend. I was wondering, have you have seen her?" The individual held out his iPhone for Kovac to look at it.

He made it a practice to keep any information about guests private; it was just good business. "I'm sorry, but even if your friend was here or passed through here, we cannot give out that kind of information."

The stranger persisted, "Please, you didn't even look at the picture. I know she ran away, and I'm worried she will die alone, or maybe she already has."

"I sympathize with your concerns for your friend, but again, there is nothing I can do. If there isn't anything else you need from me, please excuse me."

Kovac pulled an April move and walked away before the gentleman could harass him further to violate someone's privacy. The chances of him having seen whomever he sought were slim, but even if he had, telling him anything was impossible.

People stay in hotels for recreation reasons, but sometimes they are fleeing from a dangerous situation. He wouldn't ever risk sending someone back into danger.

Chapter 17 ~ Nicole

While Nicole waited for Kovac, she walked the office that appeared in pristine condition compared to the rest of the hotel.

Two mahogany desks faced one another. One most likely belonged to Kovac and the other to April. Neither had any personal effects on the desks. Not even a nameplate. Just business papers and a computer sat on each desk.

Fancy, high-back, black leather office chairs were pushed neatly under each desk.

What caught Nicole's eye was the document hanging on the wall, encased in an exquisite, one-inch, wooden frame surrounded by red and gold double matting.

The words in the document were difficult to make out at first because of the intricate calligraphy, but once her eyes adjusted to the font, she could read it in its entirety. It was titled, *The Curse* and said:

> Lucifer ~ *"Did the Son of God say to you, 'Woe unto that man... it had been good for that man if he had not been born'."*

> Judas ~ *"He was right. It's true. I should never have been*

born."

Lucifer ~ *"If that were true, why did the limb snap instead of your neck? Why are you still laying here in this hole in one piece?"*

Judas ~ *"Because death is too merciful."*

Lucifer ~ *"Ah, so what if I offer you something other than death?... Do you know what this is?... I picked this from the tree of life before He kicked me out of the garden. Eat this and you will never die."*

Judas ~ *"How is that worse than death?"*

Lucifer ~ *"Eat this and it will curse you to walk the earth for all eternity. You will escape the fires of hell. You will never see the gates of heaven. Your curse will be to live in the same body, with the same soul, never to escape the pain and suffering of this world. Your God didn't close the garden to punish humans. He hid the tree of life and guarded it, because the only fate worse than death is immortality on this miserable planet. Night after night. Day after day. And it will never end."*

Judas ate the fruit.

Lucifer ~ *"You will no longer walk in the day, cursed to live in the dark. You will no longer only eat from the table or drink from the vine; the blood of the innocent will you crave as well. You won't walk this earth alone in your immortality. One day others will seek you out asking for your curse. There is but one way to end your curse, and that is to attempt to pass your curse along against someone's will. The curse will cease, and so will you. Your body and soul—both no more. There will be neither a place for you in heaven nor in the depths of hell... You are no longer Judas Iscariot. Choose a new name for yourself."*

Judas ~ *"From now on, they will know me as Dracula."*

Nicole shivered when the last words of the document had been read. It felt mystical, surreal, almost alive. Curious why such a masterpiece hung tucked away, hidden in the office instead of on display in the lobby. Its vibe went well with the ambience of the hotel.

Before she could ponder any further on what she had read, Kovac opened the door to the office to return to her. Only instead of joy at the sight of him, she glimpsed one of her biggest fears in the flesh—her best friend stood in the lobby. Most likely in search of her.

She looked paler than usual when Kovac looked at her. She probably even appeared faint. "What's the matter, Nicole? You look like you saw a ghost?"

After several deep breaths, she found her voice to ask, "What did he want?"

"Who?"

"The man at the counter."

"He said he was looking for his friend." Realization dawned on Kovac. "Was he looking for you?"

Nicole pulled out one of the office chairs while nodding her head. Feeling dizzy, she needed to sit down.

"I didn't tell him anything. He will probably move on to the next hotel. He didn't even book a room or anything."

"He might have seen me when you came in."

"If he did, he would have pounded on the door and demanded to see you. I know it's what I would do."

Kovac's logic made sense, but she was still worried.

"Just to be safe, I should move on." She got up, but Kovac grabbed her by the elbow before she could head out the door.

She looked up at him with tears in her eyes. "He might still be in the lobby. Why don't we wait and see what happens? We can watch the security footage on the computer monitors."

"Okay."

Chapter 18 ~ January

January Taylor had spent the last three months searching for his best friend, Nicole. January grew up in a foster home next door to Nicole. The two had never formed a romantic bond, but they were always connected at the hip. She was the reason he finished school, stayed out of trouble, went to college, and didn't end up another gone-bad statistic in the system.

She was the only person he could call family, and then one day she just left. He was pissed at her for running away like a coward. Nicole feared nothing until her diagnosis. January had planned to fight alongside her and stand beside her every step of the way until she disappeared.

She told him she didn't want treatments, as they would only prolong the inevitable. With their bond, he convinced himself he could change her mind. Every day with her was one more day he wasn't alone in this world. Even if death loomed certain, she should have given him a goodbye. He deserved that much.

January long ago memorized the items on Nicole's bucket list, and all the places she wanted to visit in her lifetime. Hell, he helped her write it, and she his. He imagined she wouldn't leave the country in her condition, so she would have only stuck with the places she dreamed of seeing in America. A couple of times, when he could get someone to look at her photo, he had found out he just missed her by a day or two.

Strolling through the streets of New Orleans, his gut told him he might close in on her before long. After so long without her, he'd respect her wishes not to get treatment if he found her, even to never see her awful family again, but his heart was determined to hold her hand while she passed. She would not be alone if he could help it.

He'd been to so many hotels he'd lost count. Not even sure why, he walked into the hotel with the *Unwelcome* sign outside, but he did. It wasn't the type of place Nicole would have stayed at. Frustrated that the hotel employee behind the counter wouldn't even look at his picture of Nicole, he stopped for a drink at the bar to contemplate his next move.

He sat by himself for over ten minutes, fidgeting on his phone before one of the most gorgeous women he had ever seen turned the corner. Without a doubt, she could become the air in his lungs.

Her blue hair, which was clearly a wig, he pictured ripping it off her head while she took him in her mouth. He would grab hold of her real hair and beg her not to stop.

Her white t-shirt with the words, *Alright, I'm up. Let's spread the fuckery,* told him everything he needed to know about her personality. She immediately captivated him.

"You need a drink?" she asked him. Her voice caused the blood in his body to pump straight into his dick.

"Only if you will have one with me." He flirted with her and even added a wink for extra measure. He took in a deep breath to soak up the smell of cloves coming off of her. Not caring if she noticed.

She gave him a look that said she thought he was an idiot,

but he suspected he also saw a hint of lust in the back of her dark eyes.

She didn't bother to ask him what he wanted, but poured them both a shot of Gentleman Jack, which happened to be his favorite.

"My name is January. January Taylor. What's yours?"

"No shit. I go by April. April Nikoli."

"It's nice to meet you, April."

She poured them both a second shot after he greedily gulped the first one.

"What brings you into my hotel?" April leaned against the counter and stroked the top of his hand with the tips of her finger.

Her touch sent chills through his body. "Your... your hotel, huh?"

"I am one owner. Not sure where Kovac is. He is supposed to be working the desk and bar tonight."

"If he is the brooding guy I talked to here earlier, he went into that door behind the counter."

"Brooding sounds about right. Did you rent a room for the night?"

Her questions and the third shot she poured him made him wonder if she wanted him to stay the night. It was late, and laying his head on a pillow would be necessary at some point.

"I haven't booked one yet, but I might consider it if you would pay me a visit," he told her with another wink.

"I need to see what took Kovac away from the front desk, and then we'll see," she told him, followed by her own wink.

She carried herself in a ridiculously sexy manner and was

certainly out of his league. April left the bottle of whiskey on the counter, and he helped himself, suddenly nervous because, for once, his flirting worked.

Chapter 19 ~ April

January Taylor took April by surprise. Definitely not her usual type. She wasn't overly picky with her men, but rarely did she enjoy talking to them. And this one liked to talk. She never shared her name with anyone she planned to let in her bed. Confident she would have him in between her legs before the night ended, and yet she didn't hesitate to tell him her name.

She took one look at January sitting at the bar in his baseball cap, and she knew he would be her next victim. Victim wasn't really the right word, though. She always left her partners with a memory of satisfaction and bliss.

The flirting was obnoxious—not something she normally reciprocated. Hell, it shocked her when she winked back at him. She always acted domineering, bossy, and assertive around men. Never flirted with any of them. He pulled something out of her— no one—not even her fiancé in her previous life, ever had pulled from her.

She marched into the office, prepared to tell Kovac off for leaving the front desk unattended.

"Close the door," Kovac demanded before she could say anything.

"What is going on?" April asked.

Nicole answered, "The guy at the bar. That's my best friend, and he is here to make me go home and seek treatment."

"No worries. Leave him to me," April promised. A wicked plan formed in her head. If Nicole's best friend turned, he could solve Kovac's moral dilemma of turning someone. And April wouldn't have to be the bad guy in her friend's eyes who cursed his love with immortality. Even if Nicole was hesitant to accept immortal life, she might be more inclined to listen to her best friend, especially if he, too, was a vampire.

One downside she could see included having to spend more than one night with January. There were worse things she could do with her time. And the other issue meant that she would have to be a hundred percent honest with him to keep Kovac from losing his shit.

It was time to give the art of seduction a try. April confidently shook her hips on her way back over to January. "You ready to call it a night, pretty boy?" He was a pretty boy, with his smooth skin, his baby blue eyes, and his strong jawline —outlined by a goatee that accentuated his luscious lips. His gorgeous Adam's apple kept drawing her eyes, which wasn't too far from where she would sink her teeth into him.

He gulped at her boldness. "I haven't rented us a room yet."

"You don't need to. I live here. Follow me."

He helped himself to another drink, which was probably a good thing. The more intoxicated his body, the less likely he would remember her bite.

She shoved him onto her bed without giving him a chance to second-guess himself. "April, I've never done this before."

"Don't tell me you're a virgin?" The last thing she needed was a virgin attaching himself to her romantically when her plan was complete. If she went through with her plan, she would have to mentor him, but she didn't want a lover.

"No. I mean, I've never done a random hookup."

"It's just like any other hookup. You'll be fine."

"I'll take your word for it." He lifted himself up on his elbows and confessed. "I'm a little embarrassed to say I may have drunk a tad too much. I might need a little extra help to get him hard again."

"What do you mean again?" she teased him, while carefully pulling her shirt over her head to keep her wig in place. She always assumed she got a dud sensuality gene, so it surprised her how naturally flirting with him felt. Like an old friend she felt comfortable with, or how her favorite pair of shoes kept her feet happy.

"The mere sight of you put him at attention, but the alcohol has calmed him down."

"I suppose you want me to help you out of your clothes, as well?" She would have helped him, but for the first time, she was having fun playing with a man. Fun with a human being was a foreign concept, and she wanted to explore it.

When he didn't move from his position and only winked at her with his gorgeous baby blues, she took the hint. First, she grabbed his baseball cap and tossed it over the bedpost. Next, straddling his thighs, she reached under his *Star Wars* shirt to pull it over his head.

April ran her hands up and down his chest, his abs, and down to the V at his waistline. January wasn't cut or ripped like the fireman from the night before, but he was still fit. A splash of hair decorated his chest, and both his muscular arms were covered in tattoos.

As she was about to unbutton his ripped jeans, he pulled

her down to his lips. Kissing was her least favorite part about intimacy. The expression—take it or leave it—she was always just a leave it kind of girl. It seemed too personal, too close, and she never really mastered the art of it.

January's lips on hers played like a song. The thin hairs from his goatee didn't even aggravate her like she assumed they would. His tongue sought entry and when she opened her mouth wider with permission, her heart beat faster in her chest. She caused men's hearts to speed up, not the other way around. Who was this guy? And why did he affect her so?

He unhooked her bra, releasing her breasts. When his hand cupped her breast, the pleasure became so intense she pulled back.

Feeling his manhood pressed against her, he didn't need the help he'd asked for to get harder, but she needed a distraction. He didn't resist this time when she undid his pants and pulled them down.

Grabbing his thickness, she licked the head before taking his entirety into her mouth. The few minutes she spent pleasuring him gave her heart and hormones a reprieve.

She gave into temptation to see what she was doing to him, and the look in his eyes while he watched her sent her back into heart racing mode. His breathing, heavy with pleasure, woke butterflies inside of her. A feeling she hadn't felt flying around in her stomach since before her turning.

She stopped to remove the rest of her clothes. Her emotions and desires shook her reality, but she couldn't walk away from the moment, no matter how disturbing the situation. Before she could climb on top, per her preference, he pulled her down onto her back.

April wasn't in control, but he didn't make her feel like he had control, either. It was like they were equals, both giving and taking. A warm sensation spread from the feather kisses his lips left along her body. He reached her center. She never begged a man, but she knew acutely that he had her on the verge of doing just that. Pleading with him for more and to never stop.

January watched her like she watched him. His fingers played homage to her nipples. The combination of the look in his eyes, the feel of his fingers, and his tongue moving in and out of her brought on her climax faster than she wanted.

He moved his body up, and with his tip, sought permission to enter. She wrapped her legs around him and pulled him into her in one quick motion. This time, she grabbed the back of his head to bring his lips to hers. It felt right; it felt necessary as he brought her two more times to oblivion.

April felt him tiring, on the verge of filling her. Using her vampire strength, she flipped him onto his back. April momentarily wondered if he shared moments like this with Nicole. Fury at the thought made her ride him with no mercy. She felt the urge to make him cum instead of him pumping her until he did. And he let her.

She rested her body on his. Forgetting her need for his blood. So focused on January's pleasure and what he did to her, her fangs never even made an appearance.

Chapter 20 ~ Kovac

April left too quickly, and with no kind of fight or derogatory comment, which worried Kovac. She had a scheme in mind, and he wasn't going to like whatever her plans were.

With Nicole's friend occupied for the time being, Kovac went back to work. It wasn't much that needed to be done. Just the day's paperwork had to be closed out for the day.

A hotel calendar and clock differ from the rest of the world's. Even though midnight passes for everyone else, the date doesn't change in a hotel until someone at the front desk manually changes the date to the next day.

Third-party reservations were the worst. People would show up at the front desk at 1:00 a.m. having made a reservation online for the calendar day, but what they didn't get was they just made a reservation for 4:00 p.m. that calendar day. Only reservations made online before midnight were valid to check in at the same time. While hotel time, reservations, and dates are confusing, if people took the time to read the fine print they would know the date and check in times of the reservations they made—it was clearly posted in their confirmation.

Guests didn't understand that after midnight, the room

availability was only for check in time. He could have a sold-out house on Saturday night. Someone would book a room for Sunday, and because technically it was now Sunday, they would want to check in at two o'clock in the morning, but all the rooms were full. It was a never-ending cycle and if you didn't understand the process, all you heard was the hotel trying to get one over on you.

Third-party reservation companies were a necessary evil that business owners hadn't figured out how to put out of business.

Nicole stood next to him while he argued with the couple wanting to check in because they just made an online reservation, but he couldn't give them a room because he didn't have one available until somebody checked out.

They stood there, waiting for a refund that Kovac didn't have. Another thing about third party bookings, the customer paid them; the company then sent the hotel a credit card number (not the customer's) with the funds on it. What customers didn't understand when they demanded a refund is that hotels did not have access to their credit card to return the money.

"We want to see the manager, because we are not going anywhere until we get our money back or you give us a room," the woman defiantly declared.

"I'm the owner of this establishment, and there is nothing I can do. If you want your money, call Expedia. They have your money and your credit card information," Kovac politely told them for the third time. His face said one thing while *fuck it all* was on repeat in his head.

This was one of those moments where it took all of his willpower to keep from jumping the counter and sucking them both dry. If he could give them a room or their money, he would, but his hands were tied because they'd booked through a third-party and didn't read the reservation details.

After staring them down, the pair walked over to the bar and took a seat. Kovac ignored the two while he finished the day's books.

Nicole turned her back to them. She didn't want to agitate them further by laughing in their faces. She clearly understood his explanations and found their stubborn ignorance hilarious.

Her take on the situation calmed the raging beast inside him. Hearing her laugh brought a smile to his face.

She positioned herself to look at him. His profile was the only part of him in her view, but she still told him, "You definitely should smile more."

Turning to look into her eyes, he brushed his lips over hers, the moment gone when Nelly made her nightly visit through the lobby.

Nelly strolled along, talking to herself like usual. Dialogue with herself included three different individuals she appeared to have conversations with. She would say something looking to one side of the room, then she'd answer the imaginary voice on the other side of her, and next the one in front. Occasionally, she would have to turn around because a fourth voice would enter the conversation.

"Good evening, Nutty Nelly," Kovac called out to her. She glanced at him before continuing her discussion with the voices. She never talked to him or anyone else on the property.

Nicole asked him, "Do you know her?"

"She's our resident homeless person. The employees nicknamed her Nutty Nelly. We tried to shorten her name to just Nelly, but the nickname kind of stuck. She doesn't even acknowledge anyone who just calls her Nelly." He looked cute running his hands through his hair, embarrassed he allowed people to use a derogatory name for the woman.

"She looks like she needs help. Maybe a hospital even."

"She's harmless. We've tried talking to her, but she seems incapable of holding a conversation with actual people."

Nicole watched the woman closely, who now battled her voices in a heated argument. Nelly twitched her head at one point, like she might have been trying to shake off one or more of the voices.

"Have you called the police?"

"We did every night for the first week we were in this building. It didn't do any good. She kept coming back. We can't figure out how she gets in, because we have never seen her come in through any of the doors or leave. April and I suspect there is a secret passage or entry that she comes in and stays in. We have searched for it, but can't find it."

"Have you followed her? Maybe she will lead you to it."

What Kovac couldn't tell Nicole was that Nelly would appear at night, roam for a while, and didn't disappear to her hideout until the daylight hours. Kovac and April could follow her around during the day, but their bodies demanded sleep during the sunlight hours. Neither worried enough nor cared enough to use the little energy they had at that time of day to follow her.

"Not sure how she would react to being followed. She caught a guest look her way one time, and she went off on him. Yelling at him, 'Take a picture, it will last longer.' He had been drinking and yelled back at her, 'Lady, what's your fucking problem?' The two of them went on like that until he walked away. We give her space, and she leaves everyone alone."

Kovac meant it, too. They declared her off limits to the vampires who frequented the hotel. Last thing anyone needed was a crazy lady screaming about being bitten all the time.

"What about food and clothes?" Nicole's heart felt truly concerned over Nelly, whose clothes appeared tattered, torn, and filthy.

"She doesn't ask anyone here for anything. I assume she finds food somewhere. Every couple of months, she comes in wearing something different. My guess is she goes to a shelter or one of the homeless charities for things."

"I wish I could help her." Nicole's kind heart was on display for him to see, which pulled at his heart.

"We are helping her. She has shelter every night. Not being able to communicate with her makes anything we could do for her impossible."

"What if you left food and clothes for her?"

"Where would I leave them? Even if her mind could grasp I left something for her, would she then take anything that was left lying around? She might start stealing guests' belongings then. We always have coffee in the breakfast area, and the staff know not to kick her out if they see her grabbing something during breakfast. She might eat then, but I've never seen her there."

Nicole dropped the subject, but continued to watch Nelly, who found a seat at the guest computer and then talked to the blank screen like she'd found an old friend to commune with.

Kovac finished his paperwork for the night, Nelly stayed at the computer. The couple still sat fuming at the bar, and Nicole patiently hung out with him for his entire shift.

"Are you and April the only two who work the night shifts?"

"No, we try to keep two employees to share the night shift with, but it's hard to keep night auditors. The hours are brutal on people. We only have one on payroll right now. April and I split the nights that our employee has off."

"When is your next night off?"

"I still have two more shifts after tonight. Our employee works eight nights and then gets six off. April takes the first three, and I take the next three. If April had to deal with people any more than that, she might kill someone."

Nicole probably thought he jested, but he indeed spoke with all sincerity.

Chapter 21 ~ April

January passed out in her bed, leaving April to enjoy her clove cigarette and watch the sunrise.

She would have kicked him out of her room, but she needed him for her mission: *Give Kovac A Happily Ever After*. Except... the man awakened something in her that died in her human life. The jumpstart of her heart put a damper on her less-than-perfect plan.

With the sun up, she climbed into her bed beside January, accidentally waking him up.

"How long did I sleep?"

"Less than an hour."

"I need to go." He tried to leave, but she couldn't have that.

"What's the rush?" she asked him, while he pulled his pants on.

"I'm looking for a friend, and I need to get back to it."

"I know where she is," April confessed.

January stopped putting his clothes on. He looked at her in confusion. "How do you know where she is? I never even showed you her picture."

"She was downstairs and saw you when you came in. She's hiding from you," April nonchalantly told him.

He turned to leave. "I need to see her."

"She doesn't want to see you."

"I don't care."

"You know where she is. She is not going anywhere unless you scare her into leaving. Come back to bed, and together we can come up with a plan so we all get what we want."

January took his hand off the door handle he had grabbed to go search for Nicole. He turned to look back at April. She was playing with her breasts, hoping to appeal to his hormones to get him to stay.

"What's in it for you?" he suspiciously asked.

"Look. I don't want Nicole to run again any more than you do. Trust me. Can you do that? I'll explain everything to you after I get some sleep."

Cautiously, January nodded his head, stripped down to his boxers, and climbed back into April's bed. He kept trying to quiz her, but she refused to be drawn and told him to sleep, and they'd work it all out later.

It relieved April when he rolled over on his side of the bed without trying to spoon her.

She laid there, struggling to fall asleep, listening to his peaceful breathing. April weighed her options. Should she tell him everything right away, or should she earn his trust first? She wasn't sure if she'd tell him the whole ugly truth or paint it like her maker painted it to her. Kovac would feel the need to kill her, no matter which story she told January.

April succumbed to sleep before deciding on what words

to say to January to guarantee Kovac's dream come true. She was better at winging things, anyway. She'd worry about it after she woke up.

Chapter 22 ~ January

January woke up before April. He sat on her balcony, smoking one of her cigarettes. It tasted interesting. The smell was heavenly, reminding him of the vixen sleeping behind him, yet it burned his lungs with each drag.

His desire to find Nicole should have had him knocking on every door in the hotel, but his gut told him to wait and see what April had to say.

To take his mind off Nicole, he thought back to the night's wild sex. Having only been with two other women, who were both girlfriends, last night's sex was like nothing he had ever experienced before.

His and April's bodies fit like they were made for each other. It baffled him—she was a complete stranger, yet he felt connected to her in the depths of his being.

Her layers of armor she wore around her countenance, he longed to peel away one section at a time. Even if she kept the armor on for the rest of the world, he wanted to be the one to see sides of her she never revealed to another soul.

January had been awake for a couple of hours before April stirred. Thinking about her for those hours emboldened him to act without reservation.

He hadn't eaten in nearly twenty-four hours, and his stomach growled. But what he craved at the moment laid mostly naked under the sheets. With assertive confidence, he yanked the sheet off of her, followed by her panties. Her opened thighs were an unspoken invitation for him to take her.

January didn't ask for permission when he dove in between her thighs to enjoy her sweet nectar. Her throaty moans encouraged him to continue.

He pushed first one finger and then a second into her hot sheath while she grabbed his other hand, filling it with her breast. He didn't stop until she gripped his fingers with her orgasm.

When she stopped trembling, he removed his boxers to release his throbbing erection. Confidently, he sat against her headboard. Sitting there stroking himself in invitation for her to ride him.

April's grin was nearly enough to make him explode in his hand. He watched her closely as she impaled herself on him. She sat perfectly still long enough for her to open up enough to take all of him.

She rode him, her stallion, and took him like an experienced cowgirl. January paid equal attention to her breasts that were level with his face.

When she came again, she screamed in pleasure while pulling every drop of his seed from him.

April pulled his face to look at her, revealing a set of fangs that only existed in the movies. Yet he knew they were real. And her eyes had turned the color of blood.

He wasn't afraid; it was intoxicating. On instinct, he turned his neck, inviting her to drink from him. Her fangs pierced his skin. She pulled the blood from his veins while his cock still filled her. It was a form of intimacy beyond words.

His body was ready for round two after she'd licked his wound closed. Flipping her over onto her back, he drove into her, hard and fast. The headboard banging into the wall. But neither cared if a neighbor heard.

He willed himself not to pass out from the loss of blood and the exertion he put his body through. Passing out would have prolonged the answers he needed.

Lying beside her, when she said nothing, he said, "I'm guessing vampires are real?"

Quietly, almost in a whisper, she told him, "Vampires are real."

"Is that your plan? Are you going to turn Nicole into a vampire?"

He waited patiently while she formed the words to say what she promised him last night.

"Kovac is like my brother. He's my best friend, and a vampire like me. You met him last night at the front desk. He's over a thousand years old. The only thing in this life he has ever wanted, but denies himself, is a life partner. See, we can't make anyone a vampire unless they let us. Free will and all. Most think immortality is a gift, but it's actually not. Our souls are prisoners in these bodies, stuck on this crappy planet for all eternity. Kovac refuses to curse anyone. I can see he already loves her, but his conscience won't let him even give her the option. As his best friend, I want him to find someone. He is the one soul who deserves happiness. Kovac will probably hate me forever, but when you showed up, my mind went to work on how you could help me—to help them both."

"What's in this for you?" January asked her.

"Kovac is the only one I have ever loved. He is my family, but I'm a lone wolf. I want solitude, traveling, and freedom. I won't leave him alone until he has someone."

"What's in it for me?"

"You won't have to watch your friend die. If you want this curse, I'll give it to you. Giving it to you might be the only way to turn her, and if I do, Kovac might never forgive me. As much as he wants her, he might not get past his morals to accept the gift she could be to him."

"I need to think about it."

"Of course."

"What is the plan to get her to agree to see me?"

"Tell me why you're here, and what you want from her. I'll talk to her for you. She might take it better coming from someone else."

"Does she know you both are vampires?"

April shook her head.

"She refused treatments. I get that now. At first, I didn't. I tried to talk her into doing them. I told her it was selfish for her to not give me as much time with her as possible. So she ran away. I understand that I was the selfish one. I don't want her to die. I've had to come to terms with her dying the way she wants to, but I can't accept her going through it by herself."

"She's probably with Kovac. I'll get a shower and then talk to her. It might take more than one try. Can I tell her you promise to stay away while she thinks about it? And that you will leave if she wants you to?"

"I can't promise to leave."

"You don't have to keep the promise. Just making the

commitment might win her over."

"I can agree to that."

She got out of the bed to clean up and grabbed some fresh clothes.

"Want to join me?"

Turning down a wet, naked, sexy woman in a shower— was an impossible feat for any man.

Chapter 23 ~ April

After the best shower of her life, April threw on a pair of jeans with her shirt that read, *I would like a quick shout out for not hitting anyone with a chair in the face this week. Believe me, it's pure willpower.*

She also slipped on her layered, neon green wig, having taken the blue one off for her shower. January should feel privileged to be the only man in decades to see her with her natural hair, which grew thin and scraggly. If her talents included communication, she might have told him so.

January had lots of questions for her, and she promised to answer them all after she'd talked to Nicole and Kovac, who she assumed she would find together.

She knocked on Kovac's door first. When he didn't answer, she tried Nicole's room next. Nicole opened her door, looking more radiant than usual. April labored under the opinion that Nicole needed Kovac as much as he needed Nicole. Maybe they were wrong, and a vampire could find a soulmate.

"May I come in?" she asked when Nicole stood there saying nothing.

"Sure. Are you looking for Kovac? He's not here."

"I was looking for both of you, but mainly you. Mind if we sit on the balcony so I can smoke?" April headed to the balcony without waiting for Nicole's response. She felt nervous, and she didn't get nervous—ever. After a few drags, she calmed down enough to bring up January.

"He just wants to share the time you have left. He promises not to ask for anything other than that."

"You told him I'm here!" Nicole exclaimed with panic in her voice.

"I believe him. He said if he breaks his promise, you can tell him to go home and he will, but that you shouldn't be alone."

"I need to think about it."

"That's fair. I'll keep him away from you until you say different," April assured her but didn't get up to leave.

When April lit up a second cigarette, Nicole asked her, "How is he doing?"

"He misses you."

"That's my point. He has been mourning me for months. How can I let him back in my life only for him to lose me again?"

"Not knowing if you are dead or alive prevents him from moving on. He will live with that grief forever." April surprised herself with the bit of wisdom she spewed.

"I still need time to think about it. Tell him I'm sorry, and I love him."

"I will," April promised, and this time she took her leave.

Chapter 24 ~ Nicole

Nicole waited for Kovac on her balcony. He'd promised to pick her up so she could join him for his shift.

If she wasn't a selfish coward, she would have agreed to see January without taking the time to torture herself over the decision.

The reality was that her entire journey into the afterlife focused entirely around her. And why shouldn't it? She was the one going through it, not anyone else.

Kovac knocked on the door they shared, shaking her out of her guilt-ridden thoughts for the time being. They would plague her again later, but she needed to live in the moment. And with Kovac was the moment she wanted to live in.

The day after tomorrow, once he wasn't working the desk, she planned to ask him to make love to her, so she wouldn't die a virgin.

When she opened the door for him, he greeted her with that smile she loved so much. He didn't wait long before he pulled her to him for an earth-shattering kiss.

Embarrassingly, she let out a small whimper when he

stopped the kiss because they needed to head downstairs to relieve the person working the desk.

Kovac acted like a gentleman and pretended not to hear her, but she felt confident he did.

Was it too soon to fall in love with him? She'd never been in love, but what she felt with him had to be love. What else could it be?

They walked hand in hand downstairs to the lobby. Standing at the front desk was a man, stark naked. He appeared older, possibly a retired marine, based on his physique and the *semper fidelis* tattoo on his left forearm.

Kovac released her to see if he could help with the situation. "Can I help you, sir?" he asked while looking around for Roger, who should have been at the desk.

The man turned around in all his glory to answer Kovac. "I locked myself out of my room."

"And how did you manage to do that?" he asked the guest, who was certainly intoxicated based on his slurred speech and bloodshot eyes.

"I thought I was going to the bathroom, but ended up in the hallway. The door locked behind me."

Nicole stood off to the side, desperately trying to hold in her laughter but failing. Kovac gave the man another key before he headed back up the stairs for any to see that walked by.

"Is that a first?" Nicole asked.

"It's New Orleans—the party city. With all the drunks around here, it happens frequently. Sometimes they have just a shirt on, other times just underwear. It's even occurred more than once in an evening. I don't know why, but it's always men. I've never had the privilege of encountering a woman walking the halls without her clothes. Never a dull moment, that's for sure."

Roger turned the corner, interrupting them to say, "Sir, we have a problem in room 110."

"What's the problem?"

"I was doing room checks to make sure everyone had checked out and housekeeping had cleaned all the rooms." He stopped talking as if he was afraid to say what he needed to say.

"Well, what is it?" Kovac pressed.

"There is a dead body in the bed," he finally admitted.

Exasperated, Kovac asked, "Nicole, can you wait behind the desk? Call April's room and ask her to come help. She's in room 213."

She nodded at Kovac, but he had already turned to go see about the body.

Chapter 25 ~ Kovac

Anytime they found a body in his hotel, Kovac's stomach hit the floor. Just this once, he hoped they had died of natural causes, but they never got that lucky.

The murderer had posed the body like a mortician poses bodies in a coffin. His hands folded neatly over his chest. Obviously, someone had drained him of all his blood.

Vampires signed a contract to stay in his hotel. The document clearly stated if the death of a human occurred by accident—as long as the culprit turned themselves in—neither Kovac nor April would call the hunters. Failure to report the incident to Kovac or April meant the vampire suspect would be put on the vampire hunters' wanted list.

No denying the man had been dead since last night, and the vampire who did this to him fled. He picked up the phone in the room to call the local hunter.

After a couple of rings, Bobby Faciane answered his phone.

"We have a situation at the hotel" were the only words Kovac said before hanging up.

Bobby wouldn't take long to get there, and Kovac needed

to send Roger home. Roger would notice that he didn't call the police if he stuck around and would bring up questions Kovac couldn't give him answers to. Roger insisted on staying to help with the police, but Kovac easily convinced him he didn't want to get tied up with the police for the next several hours.

Back in his office, Kovac pulled the records and picture of the vampire in the adjacent room to the victim. Along with the human's name for the family notification.

Vampire hunters didn't go through legal channels when a vampire killed a human, but they had the means to notify the family and explain the cause of death in a way the family felt satisfied. Somehow, they had connections for the bodies to get sent to the proper funeral homes as well.

Kovac never learned the ins and outs of vampire hunter laws and ways. He just made sure he stayed on their good side.

Nicole and April were hanging out while he gathered everything he needed for Bobby.

"Send Bobby to room 110 when he gets here," Kovac instructed April.

Kovac wanted to check the vampire's room in case he found her holed up in it still. Searching the room didn't take long. The vampire checked in under the name Cinder. Records listed her as a first-time visitor, and it would be the last visit to his establishment.

Cinder must have packed up her stuff and ran as soon as she'd killed him. There were no signs left of her in the room and housekeeping had already cleaned it.

Bobby showed up as Kovac left the room Cinder had stayed in.

"It's never good to see you, Kovac," Bobby Faciane told him.

"I know."

"So, what do we got?"

"Male victim. Guest registration says his name is Lee Holloway. Vampire culprit I have registered as Cinder." Vampires only used last names for human purposes, and he didn't require one for a stay in his hotel. First name and the snapshot he took at check-in had always been enough for the hunters to put out their version of a warrant for the capture of the vampire unable to control their thirst.

"Did she let you know what happened?"

"No, we found him like this. She ran."

"Did she leave anything behind?"

"Nope, just checked before you got here."

"Okay, well, I'll get Mr. Lee out of here. It goes without saying. Call me if Cinder returns."

"I will," Kovac promised.

It didn't take too long for Bobby and his people to move Mr. Lee Holloway's body out of the hotel.

Kovac wanted to put the incident behind him and dreaded coming up with a lie to explain the body to Nicole.

Chapter 26 ~ January

Waiting for April to get back, January worked on the list of questions he had. The list wasn't very long because his thoughts kept coming back to the most wickedly beautiful and fascinating woman he had ever met.

His biggest question being, was April a murderer or one of those good vampires who only drank animal blood like on TV? She'd drank his blood, so she didn't just drink animal blood. She didn't kill him, he assumed because she needed him.

He stress-ate the entire box of pizza he had delivered to the room.

When April opened the door, his stomach twisted in so many knots that he had to run to the bathroom to expel the excessive amount of food he had consumed.

"Was it something I said?" April asked, while leaning against the doorframe of the bathroom. He knew if he looked her way, his desire for her would win out over his need for answers.

With his head still hung over the toilet, he asked her, "Do you kill people? Would I have to kill people? Would Nicole have to kill people? Because she would never agree to that."

"And you would?"

"I'd kill for her. If it meant saving her," January admitted.

"You don't look like someone willing to kill for anyone."

"I would do anything for her."

"Why? Are you in love with her?" April's tone sounded jealous in his ears. Or maybe it was wishful thinking on his part.

"I'm not in love with her, but I do love her. She's the only reason I have survived this long."

There was more to the story hidden behind his words, but she didn't ask for it. He kind of hoped she would have.

She sat down on the floor across from him because he still hugged the toilet with his body.

"Just like there are good humans and evil humans, there are good vampires and evil vampires. We only need—at the most —a pint of blood at a time and sometimes a taste is sufficient, so killing someone is never necessary."

The weight fell from his shoulders. The idea of drinking blood definitely felt weird, but agreeing to kill innocent people might be a burden he wasn't sure he could agree to. Even though he said he would do anything for Nicole, he wasn't sure he meant it. Self-defense was one thing, but murder did not fit with his nature.

"Can you be killed?" he asked.

April shook her head. "Nothing kills us. The only way to stop us is to entomb us."

"Are there vampires entombed somewhere?"

"Yes. A vampire killed the guy downstairs. If a hunter finds her, they will bury her alive for all eternity."

"Do these vampire hunters hunt all vampires or just the

116

evil ones?"

"Just the evil ones."

"How old are you?"

"Over three hundred years old."

"Wow, where were you born?"

"New York."

"What about Kovac? How old is he? Where was he born?"

"He's over a thousand years old and his native home is someplace that doesn't exist anymore. From what he told me about it, my guess is it was located close to Russia somewhere."

"Have you ever turned anyone?"

"I never wanted the responsibility."

"What is the responsibility?"

"As someone's sire, you agree to mentor them, care for them, and guide them as a new vampire. Usually, a familial bond is formed. You are forever connected to them."

"Where's your sire?"

"I woke up after he turned me, and I couldn't find him. He had disappeared. I don't know if he abandoned me or if something happened to him. Kovac found me and acted as my adopted sire."

"That explains why you care for him so much."

She didn't respond to his statement. January noticed she avoided any subject involving who she was as a person or feelings of any nature.

"Are you dead?" he continued with his line of questioning.

"No. My heart still beats, my blood still flows in my veins, I still have air in my lungs, and my soul's trapped in this body that can't die."

"You sleep during the day. Does that mean sunlight can hurt you?"

"It burns like a severe allergic reaction. It might cause your skin to fall off. No one can withstand the pain long enough to find out. But it won't kill us."

"Do you only drink blood? Can you eat regular food and stuff?"

"Blood is just an addiction. We can't quit. It's like a wicked high, but it doesn't sustain us. Food and drink are still something we can enjoy."

"Is April your real name? It doesn't seem like a common name from three hundred years ago?"

"That's part of the curse. A person's identity is nearly as important to them as their free will. Your first act as a vampire is to choose a new name, saying goodbye to the identity you have always known. You are no longer who you were before, but someone else."

"Then what was your name before?"

"Saying goodbye to my human life and my identity was painful. The only way to get over it was to forget my old self and focus on the new me. The old name is long gone—you don't need to know of it."

"Does the transformation hurt?"

"Worse than anything you will ever experience."

"When you willingly became a vampire, did you know what you were becoming and giving up?"

Looking down at the ground, she shook her head. "I didn't ask any questions. I just agreed because death terrified me. Fear is the strongest motivator for a human."

"What is your plan to give Nicole this choice?"

"I could tell her everything, but I am nobody to her. You need to tell her or convince Kovac to get over his fear of cursing her to do it himself."

"Why me? Why turn me?" he asked her again. Even though she gave him the answer earlier, he needed to hear it explained one more time.

Patiently, she answered his question again, "To sweeten the few perks of immortality. Maybe her and Kovac can live happily ever after, but it's still a new relationship with no guarantees. With you, though, you have always been there for her, and can still always be. No one wants to die, but Kovac will do everything he can to talk her out of immortality because of how he feels about her. He already cares deeply for her; he might even love her. She is the first human who has the real possibility of being the lifelong companion he desires."

"How long are you stuck with me if I agree?"

"It takes at least a hundred years to learn control over the bloodlust."

"And you would put up with me, a stranger, for that long just so Kovac could have companionship?"

"It's a small price to pay for the only person I have ever loved to have a chance at happiness."

"How can I be sure you won't leave me once you tire of me?"

"It's true. I am a bitch. I hate people, especially stupid people. I have no patience or tolerance for pretty much everyone. I don't do feelings. I have no regrets. I say whatever the hell I want. Always have and always will. Now that you know who I am in a nutshell—blatantly honest—I assure you I would never leave someone the way my sire abandoned me."

Chapter 27 ~ April

April shared more with January than she had ever shared with anyone. She and Kovac didn't even have conversations with such intensity.

When it seemed January would not ask any more questions at the moment, she looked over at him to ask the question that had been burning inside of her. "Why weren't you afraid when I showed you what I am?"

He seemed to debate his answer. After careful consideration, he lifted his head away from the toilet to meet her eyes. Taking a deep breath, he spoke truthfully when he told her, "I felt too captivated by the most beautiful creature I had ever seen to feel fear. With our bodies still joined, I felt connected to you in such a way that I knew I had nothing to be afraid of. In that moment, all I wanted was all of you."

The truth he expressed in his words crawled inside of her and buried itself deep into her heart. A heart she kept closed since the man she thought she loved refused to join her in immortality. She suspected long ago she'd never loved him. Since meeting January, he'd confirmed her suspicion.

Not that she loved January, but her feelings for him went

deeper than anything she'd felt for the one who'd ran screaming in terror when she revealed the truth of what she had become.

If she didn't get some air, she might shed a tear. Her tears she'd locked up tight since Kovac saved her. And releasing them never played a part in her plans.

Getting up off the floor, using her vampire speed, she ran to her balcony. Holding the wrought-iron railings, she fought to calm her breathing.

January followed her. His watchful eyes upon her from the shadows of her balcony entry rose goosebumps across her flesh. She could appreciate his silence as he respectfully waited for her to process what he admitted to her.

She turned in search of her cloves. January had one in his extended hand. He already knew what she needed. She accepted the cigarette with a shaky hand and brought it to her lips so he could light it for her.

The wind blew the smoke from her first drag in January's direction. Unprepared, his lungs rejected the smoke, bringing on an uncontrollable coughing fit.

The human action gave April time to put her emotionless mask back in its proper place.

With January's lungs recovered, he stepped out onto the balcony, took a seat, and lit a cigarette for himself.

She needed to get him a room of his own or the walls would close in on her, stealing all sense of control.

April reached for another clove when January spoke his concerns. "If I can turn your world this upside down in twenty-fours, how will you put up with me for a hundred years?"

With her walls fully in place, her crimson eyes found his crystal blue eyes. "I'll survive. I always do."

Tossing the half-smoked clove in the ashtray, April stood up and began stripping her clothes off. "I'm done talking."

January didn't have to be asked twice when he stood up to remove his clothes, too. In his birthday suit, he sat back down in the patio chair. He grabbed her hand and pulled her body onto his. Dripping wet, she slid down easily on his ready cock.

Again, he turned his head, giving her permission to drink from him. She sank her fangs into his willing vein. The second taste of his blood filled her mouth. He was sweet, yet salty. January's blood spoke of his surrender to her. He belonged with her and she with him. The pleasure in the truth running down her throat brought on an unprecedented climax. The walls of her channel gripped tightly around him, pulling him deeper inside of her.

In that moment, she could offer him her blood and he would accept it without question. But he needed to see and talk with Nicole first. If she chose death, January would despise her for his immortality. His rejection she might never come back from.

Chapter 28 ~ Nicole

Kovac's explanation for the body found in his hotel had only been half of the story. He didn't fool her. Nicole, being consumed with her own mortality, couldn't find it in herself to care that he left her in the dark. She had enough worries of her own, making bothering with the occurrences of others inconsequential.

January's unexpected arrival consumed her thoughts. He never lied to her. Confident of the truth in his promises, she decided she would see him. She just wasn't ready to admit it. He was the boy next door, her protector, her friend, and the only one who ever looked out for her.

She wasn't lying to Kovac when she'd told him she ran away from her family, but she didn't tell him the whole truth. Her birth mom died in a car accident during Nicole's childhood. The circumstances around her mother's accident were kept from her. When she first received her diagnosis, she decided she had to know the truth about her mom's death. It took a court order, but she obtained access to the police and coroner reports. According to the coroner's report, her mom had cocaine in her system when she ran her car off the bridge.

At the time of her mom's death, her parents had already

been separated for years, failing to finalize a divorce. Her alcoholic dad lived with his alcoholic girlfriend, whom he married the day after they put her mom in the ground.

Nicole's new stepmother had two small boys. Her stepmother took charge of every decision ever made in that house, because her dad had no balls whatsoever.

Her dad and stepmother were what society called functioning alcoholics. They went to work every day and drank all night long. The needs of their children never came into consideration.

About a year after the death of her mom, January moved into the house next door. The couple there took in foster kids for the money. They had six to eight kids at any given time.

One night she lay on her back looking up at the stars when January joined her and introduced himself. It would be the start of the only healthy relationship she'd ever had.

Their bond soldered into a kindred bond. A romantic attachment never formed for either of them. Watching movies together as teenagers, they saw enough best friends find a happily ever after that they discussed trying because it made sense. They were each other's first kiss. It only took the one kiss to know the pair were never destined to be lovers.

The note she left her family read, *Hopefully, I don't see any of you on the other side.* It was in stark contrast to the one she left January: *I'm sorry. I didn't know how to say goodbye. May we meet again. I love you.*

Leaving January, the pain raked through her more deeply than the day she received her death sentence.

Kovac left her to her thoughts until the Thai food he ordered arrived. He enjoyed his yellow chicken curry and rice, while Nicole pushed around her beef pad see ew.

"Do you want to talk about it?" Kovac asked her.

"April told January that I'm here. He wants to see me but will wait for my permission."

When she didn't continue, he asked her, "Is this one of those moments when I am supposed to nod and listen, or do you want my advice?"

His question put a smile on her face. "Just nodding and listening is good."

Kovac had finished his dish when Nicole put her first bite in her mouth. After three bites, she closed her food up and pushed it away.

"I'm going to see him. Maybe say goodbye in person. He promised not to ask anything of me except to be here. I've never known him to go back on his word."

She noticed the jealousy in his voice when he asked, "Were you two a couple?"

"Only friends. My family history is tragic. I will remember January as the only good thing I had in this life. We aren't blood, but he is the only one who treated me the way family should. That's all I'm going to say about my family. I really don't want to talk about them."

"We don't have to talk about anything you don't want to talk about."

"Will you stay with me when I see January?"

"I'm not going anywhere unless you tell me to."

"I should probably call him and get it over with."

"Have him meet us at the bar. I'll pour you both some liquid courage." Kovac stole a kiss before leaving her to call April's room.

Chapter 29 ~ Kovac

Thirty minutes after Nicole called April's room, January and April met them both at the bar. His best and oldest friend never ceased to shock him with her crazy t-shirts. The one she came down wearing read, *I don't get nearly enough credit for managing not to be a violent psychopath.* What was even crazier about the shirt was the truth of that statement regarding her. If people only knew how much on the verge of exploding she continually stayed, they would avoid her at all costs.

Tonight, though, she seemed different. He couldn't put his finger on what had changed about her, but there had been a shift in her demeanor.

January ran to Nicole, pulled her into his arms, and held her tight. The friends both wept in one another's arms. Kovac poured April a shot of whiskey and vodka for himself.

He promised to stay by Nicole's side until she told him to leave. The moment made him slightly uncomfortable, as it seemed better suited for privacy. But he wouldn't break his word to her.

A blood-curdling scream interrupted the reunion and his discomfort. "I'll check it out," April volunteered.

They both knew the cause of the scream, but they still needed to pretend to check on their guests for Nicole's and January's sakes.

"How have you been?" Nicole asked January.

"Better since I found you."

Avoiding the awkward pleasantries, Nicole introduced her friend to Kovac.

January offered his hand for a handshake. "April has told me a lot about you. It's nice to meet you."

Kovac returned the handshake, lifted an eyebrow in concern over what all April may have told him, and replied in kind, "Nicole has told me a bit about you as well."

April had finished her false inspection regarding the scream to get stopped by a guest carrying a cup of coffee.

"Excuse me, miss, do you have any coffee sleeves?"

April looked the misshapen man up and down first, then made it perfectly clear what an idiot he was in her mind. "Do we look like fucking Starbucks to you?"

Not waiting for him to dignify her with an answer, she plopped down on a barstool. "Shit, Kovac, I forgot. Sorry," she told him when she realized she'd let the F word slip out to a guest.

It wasn't the first time, and it wouldn't be the last. Kovac just shook his head, trying to hide the smile. April was—well, she was April, and to have her in your life was to accept her screw-them-all attitude. Nicole and January didn't attempt to hide their giggling over her take-no-prisoner comment. Nicole looked more beautiful when she seemed happy.

Her happiness was short-lived. The excitement had been too much for her. As they enjoyed the mood-lightening moment, her eyes jerked in their sockets. It was as if she wasn't even there. She slid off the stool, her arms jerked, and soon her whole body started shaking. She was having a seizure.

With his supernatural speed, he caught her body before she fell to the floor. Gently, he laid her on the cold tiles to minimize any damage the violence to her body might cause.

"I'll call 911," January declared in a panic.

"She wouldn't want that. Give her a few minutes. Seizures sometimes pass on their own," Kovac demanded.

"Fine, but only if you give me your word you will tell her the truth and let her choose if she wants to live or die."

In anger, he turned to April. "You told him?"

She shrugged her shoulders with a what-are-you-going-to-do-about-it attitude.

"Give me your word, or I'm calling an ambulance. And I will still tell her everything myself when she wakes up." January glared at him and pushed again.

"All right. You win," Kovac reluctantly agreed.

The seizure passed the moment he agreed to offer her immortality. Kovac tenderly cradled Nicole in his arms, waiting for her to wake up. The fearful wait lasted only a couple more minutes before she stirred awake.

April handed him a glass of water with a straw in it and a cool, wet rag. His friend had the clearest mind of the three. January and Kovac panicked while April used her brain to help the situation. One reason he didn't argue with her everyone-is-a-moron-attitude had to do with the fact that she had more common sense than much of society.

Nicole opened her eyes. "What happened?" She looked at January for reassurance—the way she always had in times of trouble—and Kovac felt the sting of jealousy.

"You had a seizure. How do you feel?"

"I'm fine." She sat up. "I've just got a headache."

April turned to Kovac. "I'll finish the shift if you want to take her upstairs to rest."

Kovac didn't argue when he lifted Nicole in his arms and carried her up to her room. "I can walk," she fussed.

"I'd prefer to be safe than sorry. If I don't help you and you fall down the stairs, where will you be then?"

"Ha, ha. That wouldn't happen." She nestled her head comfortably against his shoulders, with no further argument, while he carried her up three flights of stairs without losing a breath.

He planned to tuck her in and leave her to rest, but after he placed her in the bed, she grabbed his shirt before he could walk away. "Stay, please."

Kovac kicked his shoes off and joined her under the covers. She cuddled up close to him with his arm around her and fell fast asleep the moment she closed her eyes.

When it became certain he wouldn't disturb her, he snuck away to find blood. Added stress brought on the need for blood when, otherwise, he could have waited another day or two. And drinking from her veins before he told her he was a vampire was not an option.

Chapter 30 ~ Nicole

Nicole woke up for a second time in Kovac's arms. "How long have I been asleep?"

"Just a couple of hours. Not long."

"Did you lay here watching me the entire time?"

"I'm so used to being awake at night that I can't fall asleep when it's dark out." The tilt of his head to the side gave her proof he'd told her another half-truth. She figured out his tell because he did the same thing earlier when he explained the dead body.

"I need to use the restroom," Nicole admitted.

Reluctantly, he let go of her so she could relieve herself.

She quickly emptied her bladder and brushed her teeth. She then took what January once called a hoe bath, which meant scrubbing one's armpits and private parts.

After her seizure, she needed to check lose virginity off her bucket list. Even if he hid insignificant things from her. When counting one's days, there were more important issues to focus on.

Taking a chance, she boldly walked back into her room in just her matching black lace bra and panties.

Lust filled Kovac's eyes at the sight of her in her lingerie. He clearly wanted her the way she wanted him. Yet he stopped her. "We need to talk first."

Where her seduction abilities came from, she did not know. She leaned over the bed, putting the curve of her breasts mere centimeters from his face. "Please, I need to tell you something." He barely got the words out because her almost naked body caused his head to spin, nearly out of control.

Placing the tip of her finger on his lips, she told him, "Sh. Later. I don't care if you are a cold-blooded killer. I need you to help me with something, so whatever you have to say can wait."

Hesitation filled his eyes. He hadn't given in to his lust for her and would need more convincing. She didn't care what he wanted to tell her because she was living for the moment. Kovac could tell her he had a wife and kids somewhere, and she would still beg him to take her virginity. Although she didn't believe him to be the kind of man to cheat on a wife.

Casting aside all of her insecurities and inexperience, she mimicked the lap dancers she saw on TV. Sensually, gracefully, she straddled his lap. His rock-hard appendage pressing up against her told her all she needed to know. His talk could happen later.

She began placing soft kisses on his face. In between telling him why she needed him. "If I had all the time in the world, I might want you to ask me to marry you before sleeping with you, or at least be in a committed relationship. I don't have that luxury. It's not like I have been waiting for the love of my life to sweep me off my feet and marry me, but there just hasn't ever been anyone that set me on fire. Nobody has triggered butterflies or an all-consuming need to be filled with them. Until you. I thought I had doomed myself to die a virgin because of how picky I am, but then I met you. And you pushed all my buttons. Please don't let me die a virgin, Kovac."

He'd been sitting on his hands the entire time she spoke. Letting out a guttural moan when she said please, he gave in to his need to touch her. His hands graced her thighs on their way up to her sides.

"Nicole, it would bring me a joy like I have never known to grant your request. But I already am certain I love you too much to do this for you until you know exactly what I am. If you can accept me as I am, I won't hesitate to make love to you every day for the rest of your life."

She stopped kissing him. Disappointed and hurt, she climbed off him and pulled her robe on over her body. The sting of rejection kept her from hearing the most important part of his declaration: that he loved her.

Kovac, moving at an inhuman speed, took her by the arms, and begged her, "Look at me, Nicole."

She resisted, angry because she felt rejected. He pleaded with her one more time, "Please, my Nicole, look at me."

He tried to pull her into his arms again, this time she didn't resist. Giving in, she looked up at him to meet his eyes with hers. His dark eyes turned blood red, and his incisors grew two inches while she watched in shock.

"Are you what I think you are?"

Kovac nodded his head cautiously.

"So, when I said I didn't care if you were a cold-blooded killer, I was actually right."

She should have pulled away from him the second she saw his fangs. The safety she felt inside of his arms kept her from running, screaming in fear.

"I've never killed," Kovac assured her.

Confused, she asked, "How can that be?"

"Only vampires who can't control their lust kill. A pint of blood is sufficient. There is never a need to kill."

He hadn't tilted his head when he spoke, but she still asked, "Truth?"

"I won't lie to you."

"Technically, you have already lied to me."

"Lies of omission to protect you don't count, but I promise there won't be any more of those."

"Is there anything else I need to know, or can we make love now?" Checking off this item on her bucket list became more important to her than the details of what it meant to be a vampire.

"There is more, and it possibly could change your mind about making love to me."

"If I can look past you being a vampire, what else matters?"

"I can save you. You don't have to die if you don't want to."

Nicole frowned. She was confused. It was too much to take in all at once. "Okay, we have a lot to talk about, and my head is spinning with it all. But right now, my body is aching for you. Tell me everything, but not until you've laid me down in that bed and had your way with me. No matter what I decide, I want to be with you as a human."

Kovac threw his head back. His laughter filled the room. "You are relentless, my beautiful Nicole."

Chapter 31 ~ Kovac

He told her he's a vampire. He told her he could save her, and she still wanted him.

Kovac pushed her robe to the side of her shoulder. She held her gaze on him as he retracted his fangs and his eyes went back to the near darkness that they were. His fingers thrummed the strap of her lacy bra like a bow gliding on strings.

Nicole untied the robe hiding her body. Shrugging her shoulders, it fell to the floor. With trembling hands, Nicole lifted his shirt up over his head. Her hands steadied some while she traced every inch of his muscular chest with the pads of her fingers.

After studying the feel of him, she gazed back into his eyes. Unbuckling his belt without looking, she fumbled through. She unbuttoned his jeans. Followed by the zipper. Before she could push his pants down, releasing the part of him he wanted inside of her more than anything, he lifted her up in his arms.

Her legs wrapped around his back so he could lay her down gently. "I want to see all of you," she pleaded.

"Patience, my sweet Nicole." Kovac hovered above her, caressing her face. He studied the way she looked at him. The trust in her gaze, the desire for him, the love she felt toward him shone from her eyes.

All of his convictions fell to the wayside when his lips claimed hers. It morphed into a kiss of surrender for both of them.

Releasing her lips because he wanted to taste all of her. He needed to take his time. Her body wasn't ready for him yet. She might think herself ready, but he knew better.

With his heightened sense of smell, he could smell her arousal. He'd read somewhere that they should label a man who found joy eating a woman for his own pleasure a dangerous man. As much as he wanted to bring her over the edge, he couldn't wait to taste her for his own benefit.

First, he longed to see her perfect breasts. He needed to feel her nipples against the roof of his mouth.

Seeing her laying on the pillow with her hair spread out around her, she looked exactly like he pictured. A goddess, an angel, his Nicole. What name would she choose if she accepted immortality?

Still paying homage to her perky breasts, he slid his hand down to her wet, aching folds. He pushed aside her panties and slipped a finger inside of her to see how tight she might be. She felt hot and tight. Too tight, still.

"Stop me if you feel you might climax. You should have your first one when I'm inside of you." One of his lovers had told him that a first orgasm without penetration just wasn't as eye rolling as a first one with penetration.

He could no longer resist her sweet nectar for one more moment. Gingerly, he slipped her panties off while she lifted her hips. With his manhood still trapped in his pants, he was able to restrain from exploding on himself over her sexy landing strip.

He only knew what they called the cut of her pubic area because April gave him a TMI tutorial on the subject when girls first started caring how much hair that had. Kovac never cared either way, but staring at Nicole and how sexy she looked, it ruined him for any other way.

Moving her lips apart, he first blew upon her sweet garden. The giggle from Nicole's vocal chords sounded exactly like what he wanted to hear.

"Remember, stop me before you climax." She nodded her head in understanding.

Kovac started slow, licking the nectar that dripped onto the sheets. She tasted like heaven on earth. Better than blood.

He pushed first one finger and then a second. Opening and closing his fingers together to help stretch her vaginal entrance. He wanted her memory of her first time to be perfect and only perfect.

"Stop, stop." She kept her word and warned him.

He had to stand up to remove his pants. Unexpectedly, she sat up and took him in her mouth. He couldn't let her continue for much longer, or he would have filled her mouth.

Hovering over her beautiful body once more, he placed himself at her opening. "I have to go slow. I don't want to hurt you." He eased himself in a little at a time while they locked eyes with one another.

When he broke the barrier of her vaginal wall, she didn't even flinch. Still, he laid still momentarily to ensure her body was ready. Nicole began moving her hips up and down, letting him know she was all right and absolutely ready for more.

It didn't take long for the walls of her channel to squeeze him into oblivion. A younger man would have come with her, but he had more self-control than that. And he wasn't finished with her yet.

She whimpered when he pulled out of her. Lust to taste of her after her climax called to him, and this time, she didn't need to ask him to stop.

He watched her face and the contortions it made as his tongue gave her another orgasm. This time, when he pushed himself inside of her, he wasn't as gentle. Pushing her to the point of another earth-shattering explosion, he followed shortly after.

Rarely, as a vampire, did he ever need to catch his breath. Lying across her warm body, he felt winded for the first time in centuries. She did that to him.

He had exhausted her weak body to the point she could barely move. Kovac warmed a rag for her and helped her clean herself.

The sun started coming up. He laid back down and pulled her to his chest. "Sleep, now, my beautiful Nicole."

"Thank you, Kovac. I'm certain that was the best sex anyone has ever had." She fell asleep before he could respond.

Chapter 32 ~ Nicole

Nicole woke long before Kovac. He slept, unmoving. She didn't know where truth started and myth ended concerning vampires. Until earlier, she believed vampires were the stuff of legends, but here she lay next to one. She assumed his sound sleeping had to do with the sunlight still outside.

Nicole took a shower, went downstairs for coffee, and grabbed something from the vending machine to eat. Kovac hadn't budged.

Sitting on the balcony, she pondered what Kovac had told her. He was a vampire, and he could save her. Her salvation meant he would change her into a vampire like him. He'd assured her he had killed no one, and she believed him. Yet it seemed he despised his immortality.

Whatever the cons were of becoming a vampire, certainly the pros outweighed them. First, she wouldn't die when she had only just begun to live.

Thinking back on everything Kovac ever told her, she believed he wanted a life with her. She had given up on fighting for her life when the doctor informed her of the death sentence.

She remembered the document in Kovac's office. It spoke

of a curse. The drinking of blood, soul trapped, pain, suffering, changing of one's name, and more. Even with that information, she wanted to fight for a life, a life with Kovac. A cursed life seemed better than no life, and with the man she loved by her side, she felt willing to pay any price.

She'd never felt like she belonged until Kovac Nikoli entered her world.

She wasn't enough for her mother to get clean. She wasn't enough for her dad to stop drinking or to protect her from her stepmother.

January definitely held the title of the first person who ever made her feel loved, but he could not make her feel like she belonged in this world. If he did, maybe he would have been enough for her to fight the cancer. She never admitted that to him and probably never would. He didn't deserve that.

Shaken from her thoughts by the sound of music on the street below, Nicole rose from her chair to see what caused the noise.

A bride and groom danced through the street with an umbrella in one hand and a glass of champagne in the other. Right away, she knew she was witnessing the iconic New Orleans' wedding tradition.

Behind the happy couple dancing down the street, the bridal party also had glasses of champagne in one hand, but in the other they each waved a white handkerchief to the music. Following them, a marching band played "Second Line," and then the wedding guests brought up the rear with their beverages of choice and handkerchiefs flying high in celebration of the happy couple's nuptials.

Tourists stopped to take pictures and video the magnificent tradition that could only be understood in person. Having seen it on TV and read about it in books, none of them did what she witnessed justice.

Nearly twenty minutes went by before the end of the guests passed under her room. She didn't recognize the different tunes the band played after "Second Line" until the last song. "When the Saints Go Marching In," they played for the grand finale while the guests sang out the words to the song.

They appeared to be walking or dancing off into the sunset. Transfixed by the show she witnessed, she didn't hear Kovac approach. His hand on her shoulder startled her out of her bewitchment.

Nicole squeezed his hand before saying, "Good morning doesn't seem appropriate. Maybe, good day or good evening. Even better, how did you sleep?"

"I slept too good. I could get used to that," Kovac admitted while taking a seat in the chair next to her.

"It's so beautiful out here. Most think of oceans or mountains or something as beauty to behold, but here on these streets there is a different kind of beauty."

"It's why New Orleans is my favorite place to live."

"Where else have you lived?" Nicole inquired.

"Too many places to name. For now, I've settled on ten locations where my hotels are. I have to move every ten to fifteen years to hide my nature. Ten hotels gives me about a hundred or so years before returning to a city. The other cities I make home include New York City, Casablanca, Paris, Cabo San Lucas, Las Vegas, Sydney, London, Venice, and Athens. All cliché places for sure, but it's great for cover."

"I see."

Kovac appeared nervous. They watched the activity below, the silence between them tangible.

"Would you have told me you were a vampire if I hadn't insisted on making love?"

"I told you I wouldn't lie. I've thought about telling you every moment we were together since you told me you were dying. January forced my decision last night."

"January knows?"

"April told him. For over three hundred years, she has been playing matchmaker. January showing up gave her a partner to help push me to ask you to join me as a life partner."

"Why does April care so much? And I still don't see what January could do."

"The only thing I have ever longed for is someone to share eternity with. I have always refused to offer this curse to anyone, no matter how much I loved them. None of them, however, were facing death so soon. See, someone can't be turned into a vampire against their will. She knows even if you agree, I still might not be able to go through with it. And she knows I would never forgive her. My guess is she plans to turn January, so he can turn you if I can't."

"I read the curse in your office. I'm willing to pay that price, Kovac, with you by my side." Kovac looked like he stopped breathing at her confession, so she continued, "I'm a big girl. Capable of making my own decisions. I don't need protection."

"I lay dying when I accepted the curse. So did April. Neither of us were told the whole truth. I only want to make sure you are aware as much as possible of what awaits you."

"So, tell me."

"I have to go down to work soon. Come with me and I will tell you everything."

Chapter 33 ~ January

"I'm ready whenever you are." January told April while he lay beside her in the bed they had been sharing since he arrived at the hotel.

Using her speed, she raced to her balcony for one of her cigarettes. A habit, he noticed, when she became most stressed or conflicted.

She didn't care. She sat completely naked for any to see. He cared, though. She accepted the blanket he brought her to cover up with.

"Did I say something I shouldn't have?"

"No. I guess I thought it would be more difficult to convince you. You know I'm doing this for purely selfish reasons?"

"So am I. So, what's the problem?"

"Kovac and his damned conscience are getting to me, I guess."

January suspected there might be more to her discomfort than Kovac, but he had the next hundred years with her to learn the truth. She might refuse to see how good they are together. He recognized how foolish he would be to point it out. His mission, no longer only about saving Nicole for his selfish needs. If April would only give him a hundred years of his company, he would take it. A hundred years with her and an eternity without her, seemed more desirable than losing her before he had a chance to break through her walls.

"I can't explain how much it's going to hurt," she told him.

"I'm ready."

"Maybe with your dick inside of me, it will ease some of the pain momentarily." She didn't mince words and always got to the point.

"Keep that blanket wrapped around you and I will set you on this banister right now."

January pulled her out of the chair and shoved her up against the balcony railing. He slipped his boxers off and joined her behind the blanket. Foreplay forgotten when he lifted her to slide her body down on his ready dick, just like she asked for.

When her fangs slid from her gums, January pressed his lips to hers. He was overwhelmed by his need to kiss her. Slipping his tongue inside her mouth, he sliced it and tasted his blood before she did, but he didn't care. The need to consume and be consumed overpowered his entire being.

One last time, his human-self looked into her eyes before offering April his neck. Her lips brushed against his pulse before she eased her fangs into his artery. She pulled from him until he felt weak from the blood loss.

Releasing him, she didn't close the puncture. His blood slid down the side of his neck to his chest while she bit into her wrist. She didn't force him to drink. His beautiful vampire lifted her blood as an offering to him. He had to accept the exchange of blood willingly.

He pressed his lips along the puncture in her wrist to freely taste her immortality. The rotten juices from the tree of life ran down his throat. The taste was more bitter and vile than anything he'd ever known, but only briefly. It went from putrid to intoxicatingly delicious. She tasted like a mixture of cinnamon and cloves.

He gorged on her mouth-watering blood until he felt his eyes roll back inside of his head. April caught his body and dragged him inside before resting with him cradled in her arms on the floor. His screams shook the walls of the room. The last of his mortal blood forced its way out of the crevices of his form until not a drop ran through his veins.

The process was over quicker than he expected. He lay there shaking, naked, in her arms. "What name do you choose for this form?" he heard her ask him through the cloud in his mind.

"Lane." Then he passed out in the arms of the woman he loved more than anything. Even if she never loved him in return, he would love her always.

Chapter 34 ~ April

April held Lane in her arms and wept. The tears she'd held in for three hundred years flowed like a river.

Having sired no one, she did not know what to expect, but certainly what happened between them could not be normal. Something magical and mystical took place with the exchanging of their blood. Listening to his heart, it pulsed to the same rhythm as hers. There was no telling the difference. Their heartbeats were identical.

April freaked out. She knew she needed to get it all out of her system before he woke, and he wouldn't be out for very long.

To distract herself, she cleaned up the blood from his body and slipped his boxer briefs on. The first thing he would crave when he awoke would be his first taste, and he would need her to keep him from allowing the bloodlust to cause him to lose control.

Satisfied that she cleaned him all the way, she sat on the floor, leaned against her bed, and pulled his body up into her arms. She cradled him against her chest while resting her chin on the top of his head.

Every single decision she remembered making, she made

with her head. For the first time, her heart demanded control, and she had no power to stop it. Her heart insisted Lane wake in her arms.

Slowly, he stirred from his slumber. His eyelids flickered open. Eyes once bluer than the sky, now brownish black, stared back at her.

His new energy and strength sent him to his feet. "You'll be hungry. We need to get dressed," she told him.

When he didn't move to obey her, she stood up and walked toward him. Her nearness caused him to close his eyes and inhale the way she sometimes did, searching for blood.

Lane opened his eyes, now blood red, as if her blood was calling to him. "Lane, my blood won't sustain you." Before the words finished in her mouth, she felt the same desire to drink from him. Vampires don't drink from other vampires. What was happening?

Again, he closed his eyes and inhaled even deeper. "April, your blood is calling to me. It's like the nectar of the gods. I don't know how to resist it. What would it hurt for me to taste it?"

What would it hurt? Stepping closer to him, she surrendered her neck to him. Fangs never once turned her on until Lane's two-inch fangs appeared. He looked magnificent.

Gently, he punched through her skin. The experience shook through her center, causing the most powerful climax she'd ever had. *What the fuck is going on?* played on repeat in her mind.

On his own, he stopped before taking too much blood from her. His willpower acted stronger than hers because she forgot all about being the one to keep him from crossing a line.

Lane's eyes captivated her now blood-red eyes. "Want to taste mine?" he teased. And taste him, she did. Humans' blood tasted like copper and salt. She didn't drink their blood for the taste, she drank it to suppress a need. An addictive need. Lane's blood hit her tongue, and it tasted spellbinding. The taste of copper and salt replaced with cinnamon and cloves.

Releasing him, the high she felt did not consume her with guilt as the usual, but with contentment. Something she couldn't ever remember feeling.

"That was awesome, wasn't it? You taste like cinnamon and cloves. What do I taste like?" Lane asked her.

Shocked, she stared back at him. "What the fuck is going on?" she said out loud.

"Is something wrong?" he worried.

"You taste like cinnamon and cloves to me as well. I've never heard of any vampire drinking from another vampire. Never have I felt a vampire's blood call me. Also, use your enhanced hearing to listen to our hearts."

She waited for him to hear what she had heard. It took him a few moments to figure it out. "It sounds like we are using one heart. They are the same."

"That's why I keep saying, 'What the fuck is going on.'"

"Is there a book we can read? Someone we can call?"

"I don't know. First, let's test you around humans. We need to see what their blood does for you."

They dressed and snuck out a side door to avoid Kovac and Nicole. They didn't need to see Lane yet.

Walking the streets of the Quarter, she glanced at Lane as he sniffed the air around different humans. April felt nauseous. The idea of him sinking his incisors into anyone other than her pissed her off—she felt a new brand of jealousy stirring her senses.

They had been walking up and down Bourbon Street. for over an hour when she worked up the courage to ask him, "Well?"

"All I smell is copper. Like rusty copper. I can't imagine biting any of these people. What about you?"

She hadn't considered herself. Looking around, she noticed a girl in an alley—she was in trouble. Sneaking up on the perp, she used her strength to pin him to the wall. The girl ran off screaming, "Thank you! Thank you!" April licked the spot on his neck before soaking up his smell. She threw him to the ground, repulsed by his scent.

Lane stood by watching her. His fangs were on display for all to see—jealousy coming to the fore. Clearly angry and fighting for control of himself.

She pulled him deeper into the alley. "What's wrong?"

"I was ready to kill him. If you'd bitten him, I wouldn't have been able to stop myself. It felt like an animalistic instinct welling up from somewhere deep inside of me. I don't know how else to explain it." He calmed down as he explained the urges that overtook him.

She said it again, "What the fuck is going on? I hate to admit it, but I got riled up thinking about you biting someone too. Turning you has given us both a heightened sense of dominance—it's somehow given us feelings of possession for each other. We need to find Kovac. Maybe he will know something or someone with answers."

Chapter 35 ~ Kovac

On the way downstairs, Kovac and Nicole ran into a couple on the second floor. They were in a heated argument. He crawled around on the hall floor, trying to collect his belongings while she kept throwing more of his things out of the room into the hallway.

"Is everything okay?" Kovac asked the young man.

His wife or girlfriend, whoever she was, answered for him, "He's leaving. Sorry for the disturbance." She then slammed the door in his face.

The pair walked with the individual to the lobby. He went on his way with his tail tucked between his legs.

Kovac went through the motions of the shift change while Nicole found something for them to eat on Door Dash.

His nerves festered the longer they went without talking about her becoming a vampire. He didn't have any time to sit with her until the food she'd ordered arrived. She'd ordered fried chicken from Gus's World-Famous Fried Chicken.

Watching her eat her chicken legs, Kovac had to hide his laughter. Her manners were not impeccable. By the time she'd consumed both chicken legs, every finger dripped grease. She licked each of her fingers clean instead of using a napkin. Rather than feeling appalled at her lack of etiquette, Kovac wished he were her fingers.

Also, it pleased him to see her finishing her food for once. Her spirits were high, and she seemed to have more energy. A smile crept across his face, knowing all the credit went to him for bringing her happiness. He pushed aside his guilt over feeling selfish for thinking about giving her happy moments like this forever, because it meant trapping her soul.

While biting into her fries with the side of her mouth, she began asking the questions burning in her heart.

"You have a heartbeat, so does that mean you aren't actually dead?" happened to be her first question.

"You are correct, my beautiful Nicole."

"How about you tell me everything from the beginning and then, if I have questions, I can ask those?"

"Since you read about the curse in my office, I will start with the day I became a vampire.

"Where I was born, crusaders invaded our lands. It had been going on for some time. I took up the fight to protect our home until one day, an arrow landed in my gut. At that time, no one survived that injury. Lying there, dying, I felt fear like I'd never known. I shouted and pleaded for salvation. My maker heard me and offered me immortality. He didn't explain any of the consequences, and I didn't bother to ask. I just knew I wasn't ready to die.

"First, he drank from me, and then I had to willingly drink from him. The change is painful, excruciatingly painful. I wouldn't wish it on my worst enemy.

"After the pain, I had to choose a new name. Like Judas

became Dracula, I became Kovac. I thirsted for blood like the curse said I would.

"My sire, my maker, stayed with me for the first hundred years, teaching me how to control my thirst and how not to kill humans. During that first century, I experienced loneliness, but not as much with him around.

"I left him as soon as it was safe for me to be on my own. The loneliness grew bitter and unbearable at times. I sought love and companionship. First, I looked for female vampires hoping to find love amongst my kind, but most were selfish and unbearable. Later, I thought I could find a human to love and turn. I fell in love many times, but my conscience never allowed me to give them this curse.

"I trapped my soul. I will never see an afterlife free from the cares of this world." Kovac shed a tear at the end of his story.

"What happens if you die?" Nicole wondered.

"The only way out is to turn somebody against their will; by doing that, we cease to exist. You know the body we found the other day? He wasn't turned, so the vampire that killed him was unaffected. Vampire hunters will track her down and bury her alive. The other way out of this life is to attempt to make someone a vampire without their consent. Anyone who does that ceases to exist completely."

The bell rang at the desk, putting their conversation on hold.

Kovac hid his shock at seeing Cinder at the desk. She looked a mess, blood-shot eyes, cracks around the edges of her lips, and hair matted. She appeared to be in withdrawal. Based on her demeanor and appearance, she had been gorging on human blood for a while. Vampires didn't experience withdrawals so soon after drinking a man dry. Unless they drank more than needed regularly. Cinder had to be—in human terms—

overdosing on blood. She would not need a fix so soon if the other night had been a one-time loss of control. Gluttony of blood had similar effects—or worse—on vampires as abstaining.

He checked Cinder in as if nothing ever happened. She had to be desperate, coming back to his establishment. Didn't she know they would catch her? Kovac sent her to his panic room, unbeknownst to her.

Upon entering, the steel door would close her in from all sides until Bobby could collect her. The room had cameras and would alert him once the room locked her up safely inside.

Kovac followed her at a safe distance to ensure she didn't attack a human before she got to her room. Her screams, once she'd realized he trapped her, could be heard throughout the building. He left it that way for two reasons. One, so other vampires would understand he didn't tolerate murder, and two, it added to the haunting allure of the hotel.

Cinder's screams brought guests from their rooms. Nicole came looking for him, and April walked through the front doors with January.

Kovac, upon seeing January's dark eyes, turned to April. "What did you do?"

"It was his choice," she told him without batting an eye.

Kovac hadn't told Nicole about their eyes turning colors, but that obvious clue surely helped her figure out her best friend had become a vampire.

With a tear in her eye, all she said to him was, "What do I now call you?"

"Lane is the name I chose. Please don't cry for me. I wanted this."

Kovac noticed April's scent had changed, and it smelled similar to Lane's. Maybe even identical. He made a mental note to ask her about it later.

The few guests that didn't shake off the screams interrupted the foursome. "Is someone hurt?" one of them asked.

"It's just the sounds of this hotel. She will quiet down when she finishes throwing her usual fit," April assured them before offering them one shot on the house to calm their nerves.

Kovac excused himself to call Bobby.

Nicole followed him. As soon as he hung up the phone she asked him, "Lane, his eyes were almost black as night like yours and April's are?"

"Yes, all vampires' eyes are the same. Blackish brown, except when we feed. They turn blood red. It's not mentioned in the curse, so I know nothing about the how or the why."

Bobby Faciane and the rest of the vampire hunters under him walked in the door before they could continue talking about Lane.

Kovac didn't know where they resided, but he suspected the location was close by because they always made it to his place in record time.

Chapter 36 ~ Nicole

Nicole and Lane stayed in the lobby, out of the way, while April and Kovac escorted the hunters to collect Cinder.

Lane made himself at home behind the bar. Nicole didn't drink hard liquor too often, but she accepted the shot Lane put in front of her without hesitation. Lane—how long would it take her to get used to calling him by his new name?

When she didn't ask him any questions about his decision, he told her, "At first, I wanted to do this for you, but I can't pretend it didn't also become about me. The only place I ever felt I belonged was with you, but as my friend. Then I met April, and I knew I had found the home I have always wanted. No matter what you choose, I would have always chosen this path. Don't feel sad for me, please, Nikki."

He only called her Nikki when desperate for her forgiveness—or to prove his sincerity. "You are in love with her?" she asked when she realized he must be.

"Sh. Don't let her know that. She doesn't do feelings—yet," Lane told her in his cocky voice followed by a wink. He still acted like her January, which brought her comfort.

"And you think after all these centuries you are going to be the one to change her?"

"I can't explain it, but she has already changed. At least when we are alone, her walls crumble around me." His voice sounded full of confidence and so much love. Who was she to argue with him?

"I haven't told Kovac, but I knew I would let him save me the moment he told me he could," she confessed to her best friend.

Lane leaped over the counter to bring her into his embrace. No words were said between the friends, because none were needed.

Tempted to ask him what it was like to now be a vampire, but she couldn't find the words to ask him. After she'd turned, they could compare notes—the way they'd always done about their lives.

Speechless, the two watched as a hunter walked in the door, pushing a coffin. Lane poured them both a second shot of the amber liquid because of what they had just witnessed.

April joined Lane behind the counter. Tonight's choice of t-shirt read, *Thank you for making me so angry that every time I open my mouth it appears that I have Tourette's syndrome,* and she paired it with a jet-black, messy style wig. She realized with April, you never knew what you were going to get, but you were always going to get honesty. She couldn't ask for a better person for Lane. Even if she was the type of person who would have needed her own sandbox as a child because of her inability to play nice with the other kids in their sandbox.

Lane poured April a drink, which prompted him to ask her, "Can we get drunk?"

She threw her head back to let the whisky slide down her throat before saying, "Absolutely, and I'm telling you in advance, if you ever actually see me shit-face drunk, you're welcome, because I can guarantee your night won't be boring."

Nicole and Lane shook their heads, trying to contain their laughter.

"You think I'm joking. I promise you I'm not. You need to face it now. If we are going to spend the next hundred years together, you will figure out the benefits of being my friend means you will be the normal one."

"You sound quite proud of yourself?" Lane asked her.

"Damn straight I am. And why haven't you poured me another drink?"

Nicole couldn't hold her thought in any longer after Lane poured them all a shot. She'd had three shots of bourbon when she usually stuck with wine, and her tongue felt loose. "Lane, I already miss your beautiful blue eyes."

"What are you talking about?" he asked her.

After a hiccup, she told him, "Your eyes are the same as April's and Kovac's. I asked him and he told me all vampires have dark eyes." She said the last part in a whisper. Not knowing who might overhear her use the word vampire.

Lane turned to the mirror behind the bar to check his eyes out. "No shit. Look at that. Guess I left out at least one question." Turning back to Nicole, he concluded, "So, that's how you knew."

Another vampire myth debunked as she clearly saw Lane's reflection in the mirror.

A guest stopped at the bar to ask if the coffee was hot. Intoxicated, as she was, Nicole answered the woman before anyone else could, "Since you're a stranger and we have no idea what your definition of hot is, why don't you pour yourself a cup and check for yourself?" Her statement ended with an unladylike hiccup.

The liquor became too much for Nicole when she laid her head down on the bar. She fell asleep immediately.

Lane picked his friend up in his arms to carry her to her room. Kovac found them before he made it out of the lobby and took her from Lane.

Chapter 37 ~ April

The hunters moved the coffin with Cinder locked inside through the lobby and out the front door. The newly imprisoned vampire thrashed violently inside of the chained coffin. The disturbing occurrence should have caused concern amongst the people on the streets. Except it was New Orleans. Crazy shit happened there every night, and no one questioned it.

Bobby Faciane walked over to inform her they had finished. Standing in front of him, she had an epiphany.

"Bobby, I have some questions I'm hoping you have the answers to. Would you mind taking a few minutes if your men can handle Cinder without you?"

He ran his hand across his bald head, pondering the request. "I guess."

"It needs to be done in private. Let's step into the office."

He hesitated. "We won't bite, I promise," she told him.

"It's not you I'm worried about." He slowly followed them into the office. "He's new and I know nothing about him," he admitted.

With the door closed, Lane asked Bobby, "How did you

know I just became a vampire?"

"Your name appeared in our records a few hours ago. Lane sired by April. I assumed since you are here with April that you are Lane."

Full of curiosity, April needed to know. If there were records, she could find out who sired her and what happened to him. "What do you mean, his name appeared in your records? What records? How does it appear? Or is this some big vampire hunter secret?"

"It's not a secret. Your kind just rarely ask us questions. You mostly keep your distance from us. The best way I know how to explain it is to ask you if you ever heard of the *Book of Life* mentioned in the Bible."

They both nodded, so he continued, "The first hunter received a visit from an angel who told him of his destiny. This angel gave him the *Book of Vampires*, which contained instructions and a warning regarding immortals. The first name recorded in the book was *Dracula, sired by Lucifer*, along with the date. No idea how the book knows, but it does. The names show up written in blood. We have the name of every vampire ever created and who created them."

"Do you know who sired me and what happened to him?" April timidly asked.

"Kovac didn't tell you?"

The air from her lungs tightened in her chest. How would Kovac know anything about her sire? He'd never told her about him, but then again, she'd never asked him if he knew anything.

"Um, maybe you should ask him. If he has said nothing to you, he probably has his reasons." Bobby tried to get out of the situation.

April's fangs elongated in anger. "Bobby Faciane, you'd

better fucking answer my question."

Pinching the bridge of his nose while telling her, "First, put those things away, and control yourself."

Lane grabbed her hand and gave it a gentle squeeze before releasing her hand, afraid holding on to her for too long might push her away.

"The only reason I know what happened to your sire is because we have him entombed in our New York cemetery."

Sitting down in one of the chairs, she then asked, "Why?"

"The hunters had been pursuing Jacob for over two decades when he came upon you. What is the last thing you remember before you were turned?"

"Someone had broken into my home. They stabbed me in my bed. I awoke and took off running to get away. I stumbled into the alley outside my home before he found me."

"Jacob stabbed you after he murdered your neighbors. He was a psychopath turned vampire. Jack the Ripper style killer even before he had the thirst for blood. He hated being alone in his sprees, so he always had an apprentice. It was easy to capture them because they were sloppy and less careful. We caught him before he could make you his next apprentice."

April interrupted the story. Her voice cracked when she asked, "I still don't see what this has to do with Kovac and why he would keep it from me."

"Your name appeared in the book as we were closing in on Jacob. We cannot leave newborn vampires on their own or there is mass murder and chaos. Kovac was the closest vampire in the area without a protégé. We found him and asked him to look out for you."

Hurt and betrayed, she still continued to gather more information. "He didn't just stumble upon me? They forced him to look out for me?"

"He wasn't forced or coerced, which is usually necessary in these situations because there isn't a bond between the two. When they approached Kovac and told him you needed someone, he didn't argue, didn't question, he just took off as if his life depended on it. Sure, there hadn't been a natural bond formed, but he wanted you the moment he heard you needed him."

"How can you know all this? You weren't there." Tears burned behind April's eyelids, but she refused to let them fall over the knowledge Kovac never told her.

"We keep thorough documents. It's recorded."

Bobby allowed everything he told her to sink in before reminding her, "You asked me in here for a reason, and I don't believe we have gotten to that reason."

April appeared shell shocked, and Lane, knowing what her questions might be for the vampire hunter, began, "I know what she wanted, if I may?"

"Go ahead."

"All I know is what April told me about vampires before and after. When I drank her blood to turn, it was vile and disgusting, and before I finished, it turned intoxicating. She tasted like cloves and cinnamon. When I woke up instead of craving human blood I craved hers. Even though she thought it strange, she let me drink from her again. She still tasted divine. April craved my blood, too, so I surrendered my neck to her again. My blood tasted to her exactly like hers tasted to me. While I rested before I awoke as a vampire, she noticed our hearts beat in sync. We cannot hear them separate from one another. Finally, she took me out for a test. Human blood repulsed me, as did her. We also both experienced anger and jealousy at the thought of either drinking from someone else.

Have you ever heard of anything like this?"

Somewhere in Lane's ranting, without taking a breath, Bobby had sunk down into the other chair.

"There is a prophecy. One every generation laughs at as a myth. As if a hunter at some point thought to play a joke on future generations." He paused.

"What does it say?" April asked, having found her senses again.

"Let me pull it up on my phone. We actually have all our records in the cloud now. Isn't that crazy?" He chuckled nervously. It took him some time to scroll through and find what he was looking for. The two waited anxiously.

Bobby read the words in this possible prophecy. "Even in damnation there is mercy. My children will never rest in my bosom. They will never look upon my face. Fear keeps them from me. But I will not forget them. Vampires who prove their worthiness by refraining from killing will one day find their equal. They will know their equal by the identical beat of their hearts, by the matching taste of blood, and by the satisfaction of the blood that only their equal can provide. The blood of innocents can no longer quench their thirst. Man was never meant to be alone. Lucifer tricked them into choosing a life apart from me. But that doesn't mean I will ever forget them and their needs. This gift cannot be forced or sought after. An equal is only found by one worthy and should not be pursued."

The three sat dumbfounded over the words of the prophecy.

Bobby offered a possible out in case either felt they needed it. "This is a translation. The translators could have translated the original text incorrectly into the languages of the times. It's possible it's not accurate."

"It's fucking accurate," April told him as she hurried from

the room.

Chapter 38 ~ Lane

He was without a doubt April's equal, and she was his. Lane knew it before hearing the prophecy. He only understood it better after the words burned in their ears. Bobby confirmed, without a doubt, she was where he belonged.

He debated giving her space to process. Lane clearly was not part of her hopes and dreams. He understood that. After an hour on his own, he said "Fuck it" to himself to go in search of her.

Except someone looking for a room at the desk interrupted him. Kovac hadn't come back to finish the shift, and since April had run off, Lane decided to wing it.

"May I help you?" Lane asked as he headed behind the front desk.

"I'm looking for a room for the night," the stranger said.

"I'm sorry, we are sold out tonight." Lane did not know if the hotel had any availability or not, but what other options were there?

Lane moved to search for April again when the phone rang. "Hotel Lamia, may I help you?" he answered.

He heard heavy breathing on the other end before the man asked him, "I need to confirm a reservation for Wendy Toups."

Lane thought for a moment about the best way to handle the situation. "Are you Wendy Toups?" he asked.

"No, but she has reservations for your hotel. I am having a shipment of panty hose delivered to her, and I want to make sure she is staying there."

"Sir, I can't give out information regarding someone else."

"Do you wear panty hose?"

"Excuse me?" Lane asked incredulously. He had paid little attention to the background noise on the phone, but he suddenly noticed the man had porn playing on his TV.

"Do you wear panty hose? What's your favorite? Do you prefer thigh high or full figure? If the package comes, and Wendy isn't there, you can have the panty hose."

What was the man's deal? Lane hung up on the weirdo panting heavily over thinking about Lane in panty hose. It seemed the best option.

Lane desperately wanted to find April and make sure she was all right, but he thought the responsible thing would be to manage the front desk until someone came to replace him.

He knew nothing about the building, so he did his best with guests who needed things. Several stopped by for extra towels, which made him question what in the world they needed with so many towels. He successfully found towels to hand out to the guests, and after his third trip to the laundry room, he stacked several under the desk.

Many complained about the elevator being out of order, so he made up a story since it was supposed to be a haunted hotel. "Someone shot themselves in the elevator last week, and the crime scene cleanup crew hasn't been by to clean up the brain matter yet. If that won't bother you, I can open it for you." He offered the same excuse to everyone. Even added a wink after the offer, making the best of the situation by just having fun with it. No one took him up on the suggestion. They even seemed more eager to use the stairs.

Whoever said "there are no stupid questions" didn't work in customer service. The phone rang, and the man on the other end told him, "We need maintenance to fix our air conditioner."

"What's wrong with your air, Sir?"

"There aren't any buttons on the window unit, and it is hot in here."

"Are you asking for maintenance to come install buttons on your window unit?" Lane went along with the stupid idiot's questions.

"They need to do something, because I'm sweating."

Lane knew nothing about the room or the air, but he had plenty of common sense. "Did you look around the room for a thermostat on the wall?"

"Hold on, I'll check." After a brief moment of silence, the man came back to the phone. "I found it."

The night went back and forth with explaining to walk-ins they didn't have any rooms, handing out towels, explaining how to use remotes, telling people they were out of toilet paper because he couldn't find any, and other tedious activities.

The prize for the dumbest person of the night went to the lady with the missing black cat. She ran at the desk, frantic. "I have a weird question. Has anyone seen a fluffy black cat?"

Being bored in between helping people, he had read the signs posted around the desk and noticed the hotel was not pet friendly. "This is a not pet friendly hotel, and there should be no animals in the rooms," he told her.

"I looked online for a hotel that said service animals accepted."

Another bit of information he picked up from reading the signs left around for the employees helped him frustrate her more. "That being, the only recognized service animals by the Americans for Disabilities Act are dogs and miniature horses. The ADA does not approve your cat as a service animal."

"I kept her in her carrier. I only let her out to pee, and she disappeared on me."

Her whack job roommate interrupted the conversation to let them know he found the cat in the bathroom. The bathrooms in the hotel being all white, Lane couldn't imagine how dumb or how high one had to be to not see a fluffy black cat in the white bathroom.

The two crazies went on their way while the sun rose. Lane immediately felt the effects of it on his new vampire body. He wanted to lay his head down on the front desk but fought the urge.

Finally, around seven, the girl working the morning shift arrived. Lane didn't bother with a name or an explanation in his desperation to get to a bed. His body felt heavy as he climbed the one flight to April's room on the second floor.

With no response to his knocking at her door, he tried the handle. It opened. She wasn't inside. Lane felt lost and unsure of himself. He didn't have a clue where to look for her, and he felt as if his body would give out in the attempt. Reluctantly, he climbed into her bed without her to find rest for his new body.

Chapter 39 ~ Nicole

After Kovac laid Nicole in her bed, he attempted to go back to work, but she clung to him. Terrified to be alone. The seizure she experienced was her first since her diagnosis, which meant the cancer progressed.

Kovac and she hadn't talked anymore about her becoming a vampire. She knew he felt reluctant about changing her.

Lane would change her if Kovac wouldn't. She knew in her heart her faithful friend would never let her die. But she wanted Kovac to save her. To want her to share this life with him and only him. To not be able to face a world without her in it.

His reluctance weighed heavily on her heart, besides her numbered days. She understood the whole blah, blah, not wanting to curse her, but if he truly longed for a life with her or anyone, then he needed to get past that.

Immortality or her death would only be her decision, and no one else had that right to decide either way for her. It was different when death seemed the only choice. Cancer had decided for her. Now she had the power to choose death in the afterlife or a cursed immortality with Kovac and Lane. Maybe

Kovac would tire of her, but Lane would always be her family.

She and Kovac hadn't known each other long enough for love or commitment, but time was not on their side. After the turning, they could take the appropriate time required to fall in love and decide if they wanted to build a life with one another.

Nicole fell asleep long before Kovac's day sleeping and awoke with him lying next to her while the sun glared in the sky, hidden by the long, thick curtains.

A walk through the Quarter seemed perfect. Visiting shops open during business hours hopefully would not be possible for her in the very near future.

Magazine Street contained the most memorable shops. Including a store selling only antique weapons full of war memorabilia and collectibles. Nicole, not being a weapon connoisseur, still appreciated the history and beauty of each piece displayed.

She noticed artists and musicians sat on every street corner. The sounds of horned instruments brought the city to life.

The various tarot card readers intrigued her the most, tempted to have her fortune read. Fear they would pull the death card kept her from stopping. Nicole didn't need another person to tell her death was banging on her door.

She explored long into dark, lost in the city's magic. Kovac found her watching a group of performers painted from head to toe in silver paint. He saw her before she noticed him.

Sneaking up behind her, he asked, "Are you feeling better this evening, my beautiful Nicole?" She jumped, startled by Kovac's unexpected appearance that pulled her from the trance the performers had her in.

Kovac moved next to her to watch the artists along with

her. She peaked at him out of the corner of her eye. Part of her wanted to be angry at him for his position on her becoming a vampire. But the sexy smile she saw on his face in her peripheral vision wouldn't allow her to stay mad.

He reached over and laced his fingers with hers to ask, "Would you like a tour of the nightlife here in the city?"

Nicole turned to look into his mysterious eyes to say, "I've spent most of the afternoon walking around the city."

"Then you haven't seen everything there is to see. We can walk back through every place you have been to today, and it will all look different in the dark. New Orleans is very different under twinkling stars than it is in the light of day."

"Okay, where should we start?"

"First, have you eaten anything?"

She ashamedly shook her head.

"Food first, then we can explore the city after dark," Kovac semi-scolded her. "How about I take you for the best shrimp po boy in New Orleans?"

Hand in hand, Kovac led her to a place called Nola Po-boys on Bourbon Street. The sign outside read:

All our fried food is spicy.
Other options include,
    1. Yankee (Mild)
    2. Cursing Murray (the owner)
        in the morning
        (very spicy)
  All Po-boys come dressed with
  mayo, lettuce, tomato & pickle.

Kovac ordered them both a foot-long shrimp po-boy and fried okra on the side. The taste was better than she'd imagined. Clearly, it was easy to understand why New Orleans earned the accolade of being *the obese capital of the world*. Nicole barely consumed half of hers, but Kovac had no problem finishing his and hers.

Learning about Kovac, the person, proved not the easiest task. He was a quiet soul, mostly only talking when spoken to. Unless taking care of her or seeing to her needs.

"You told me about the day you faced death. Tell me about your life as a vampire in the beginning," she probed.

"My sire's name was Hynek. He rode with the crusaders invading my country. Hynek took pity at the sound of my cries and made me what I am. Ironically, a brutal killer showed me mercy. We fed on the fallen everywhere we went. Hynek left my people alone after I joined him. I told my family I'd made a deal with the enemy to keep them safe. Occasionally, I snuck off to visit them until hiding that I didn't age anymore became impossible. They would have assumed I had died when I stopped visiting.

"I stayed with Hynek for a century. Traveling the world. Not having the stomach to kill like him, he allowed me to act as a sort of servant. Cleaning the weapons, fetching water and food. The never-ending battles supplied steady blood.

"We had to move on from camp to camp to hide what we were. A war to fight loomed around every corner of Europe and then beyond. I heard Hynek's thirst for war and death eventually led to his capture by hunters."

When Kovac paused, Nicole asked him, "Do you miss Hynek?"

"Sometimes, but I don't miss the death and carnage that followed him. I felt relieved when hunters caught up to him. I don't wish entombment on anyone, but when it's the only way to stop a bloodthirsty killer, there is no other choice."

"What did you do after you parted ways?"

"I knew I wanted to live a life that helped humanity if I could. I sought a way to provide blood to vampires by lowering the risk of murder. That's when the idea for the hotels formed in my mind. They started out as inns at first because hotels didn't yet exist. The concept stayed the same over the centuries, a safe place for immortals and humans. The humans lose some blood, experience the fright they came looking for, and are otherwise unharmed. Unless a rogue vampire gets past our doors like Cinder did."

"How did you meet April?"

"I had just set up a new place in New York City. The hunters had caught April's sire because he was a serial killer—as a human and as a vampire. She needed someone to guide her as a new vampire. We have been family ever since."

Chapter 40 ~ Kovac

Kovac stood up from the table and reached his hand out to Nicole. "Are you ready to experience the night life of New Orleans? We can keep talking along the way."

She accepted his hand, which melded into his. They stepped out onto Bourbon Street. The street that overflowed with pedestrians. It had to stay closed to traffic to accommodate the people partying and hanging out.

It still amazed Kovac that despite all the people, the city's crew somehow came through every day and kept the streets litter free. In a city known for partying and tourism, one would expect it to reek of urine, alcohol, and trash. Instead, the Cajun cuisine overloaded the senses. One minute, the smell of boiled seafood wafted up the nose, and the next, the intoxicating smell of beignets filled the air.

The faint of heart or uptight should avoid walking down Bourbon Street—especially at night. Nicole tried to hold in her hysteria when they noticed the couple holding hands wearing nothing but Saran wrap. They both had a daiquiri in one hand while strolling through the night as if their attire were the latest fashion on the cover of *Vogue*.

The couple's friend, a gentleman sporting a neon green speedo and women's Gogo boots, forced Nicole to bury her head in the crook of Kovac's arm to contain her amusement.

After they were far enough away from the three bold individuals, Nicole asked, "Seriously, and the police say nothing to them?"

"What? They're covered up."

"Okay. If that's what you want to call it. Anywhere else and you might get arrested for exposure."

Nicole wanted to try the drink everyone carried around. The hurricane flavored daiquiris, the bartender poured into cups that looked like large science beakers. The twisty straws added to the excitement. Not enough alcohol in them to get a buzz. The fun look and feel of the drinks alone were enough to create an emotional high.

They avoided the buildings with pictures of naked ladies on the outside. Kovac enjoyed the smile the novelty items in the shops brought to her face. She laughed the hardest over the trick coffee cup. Customers bought the New Orleans souvenir, served their friends a cup of coffee, and when they got to the bottom, they'd find a ceramic penis staring back at them—surprise!

In one store, she fell in love with the Mardi Gras masks. Nicole tried on at least twenty different ones after Kovac insisted she pick her favorite for him to purchase. She picked out his and hers, golden masks outlined in tiny matching beads with purple, green, and gold feathers adorning the upper edges.

Kovac happily wore the mask to continue their walk through the quarter because of the joy it brought his beautiful Nicole. His self-consciousness set aside—they were in the city where anything goes.

Her cancer and the possibility of him making her a

vampire hung over them both, but for the night they pretended none of it mattered.

With a second drink in their hands, masks on their faces, and Nicole's arm wrapped in his, they fit in with the other partiers. Darkness might find them tomorrow—but tonight, everything felt perfect.

Chapter 41 ~ April

April came back to the front desk when she remembered Kovac had left and no one was taking care of their hotel.

She watched Lane handling everything from the shadows. Her soul begged her to go to him, but she couldn't make her feet listen.

When he walked to her room, she went to the front desk to mark off the room next to hers as occupied.

She climbed into the lumpy bed. Tossing and turning all day. She tried to blame it on the mattress because it wasn't hers and what she felt used to. But her heart knew she tossed and turned because Lane slept next door without her.

April felt angry and betrayed. Her eternal plans included a life of solitude, not one tied to someone forced upon her. She willingly intended to sacrifice one hundred years for Kovac to find eternal happiness, but it wasn't what she wanted.

The only man she may or may not have loved, a human, threw her away like garbage. She'd vowed then to never open her heart that way again.

Lane deserved someone who could give their everything

to him—that would never be her.

Dragging herself out of the bed when the sun went down meant she couldn't put off facing Lane much longer. Especially as a new vampire. He would need her blood.

Her body dragged like a dead man walking, heading to her room. Lane stood with his bare back to her. His hands pressed up against the wall above his head, like pushing the wall would ease his hunger. Every muscle in his back stressed as his lungs worked overtime to stay in control.

Damn her fingers that took over against her will to stroke every line of his back. "You need to feed," she told him while her hands found pleasure tracing the sides of his torso.

Lane turned to face her. His eyes were blood red, his fangs were on full display, and his venom dripped down the side of his mouth in anticipation of her blood. "I don't want to hurt you." His words came out slurred, and a tear slipped past the corner of his eye.

"Immortal here. You can't hurt me. Now drink," she commanded with her neck in submission.

His arm looped around the small of her back. Using all of his new strength, he pulled her to his chest. "That's not what I meant, and I think you know it."

He didn't give her an opportunity to respond before he succumbed to his lust for her blood. Taking only what he needed before he surrendered to his lust for her body.

Lane took what was his, according to the prophecy. He picked his equal up in his arms and tossed her down on her bed. Not caring, he ripped the clothes from her body, followed by the rest of his.

He acted like a primal animal, claiming his mate. Gently, he pushed her legs open. Her body didn't need any priming when he slammed himself inside of her ready channel.

April never allowed herself to fantasize or wish for more from the humans she brought to her bed. It never occurred to her to screw a vampire because she regarded sex as a means to an end. The end being her thirst for blood.

No man had the power to bring a scream from her throat. Until Lane—her equal. The companion she never wanted and still was not ready to accept.

For an hour, he flipped her every which way imaginable, bringing her to oblivion until she lost count. Straddling his lap while he finished. Both were out of breath.

With his arms around her back, he reached into her hair and tried to pull her to him for a kiss. April moved her head to reject the kiss. She didn't wait for permission when she slid her bicuspids into his vein to shake off the feelings trying to sneak into her heart.

It seemed inevitable she would surrender to Lane as her equal—but not today.

Chapter 42 ~ Lane

April climbed off his lap. The absence of her warmth caused an ache in the depths of his soul. Lane wondered if being a vampire heightened his emotions, besides his senses and abilities.

Hopefully, his patience held stronger, too. She would need him to dig down deep inside himself to give her all the time she needed to embrace him.

Lane didn't know if he could read her emotions because they were equals or if it had to do with his immortality.

No doubt in his mind she felt for him the way he felt for her. Only difference, she despised her feelings. Strangely, she didn't despise him, just the feelings he brought out of her.

The desire to be whatever she needed him to be for the moment guided his actions. Lane joined the love of his life on the balcony with a plan to get her mind off of the information they learned about the two of them. "Show me the sights? This is my first time in New Orleans."

The suggested distraction did what he intended it to do. April turned to him, having replaced the look of gloom with her signature "resting bitch face."

"What do you want to do first?" she asked.

"Take me to the famous Café du Monde."

April disappointed him when she headed to her bathroom alone to get ready. She didn't invite him to join her this time. He expected the rejection—yet it still stung.

The sting disappeared when she walked out the bathroom in a little, purple, chin length, layered wig. It might be his favorite. It shaped her face in a way that all of her features appeared highlighted. Her RBF had no power to hide her beauty.

Even with her fuck-humanity attitude, he still saw the hidden beauty in her that a mirror wouldn't reflect. It takes a special person to speak their mind. Like the t-shirts she sported. Tonight's read, *I don't have the time or the crayons to explain it to you.* While the rest of the world put on a façade for fear of what others think of them, April spoke her truth. She was real. She was genuine. Even more importantly, she was trustworthy—a rare quality.

Blood pooled in his mouth from biting his tongue to keep the words he ached to say to her from spilling out accidentally.

"Are you going to stare at me for the rest of the night, or are we going to go out?" April teased.

Lane offered his arm to escort her out. "My lady," he jested in return.

She accepted his arm, but told him in no uncertain terms, "I'm nobody's fucking lady."

"Yes, ma'am." The banter continued.

In the hallway they ran into a man walking up and down the hall in his whitey tighties. Clearly inebriated, even though the night had just started.

"Sir, can I help you?" April asked him.

"I'm looking for room four zero zero."

"We don't have a room four hundred. We don't even have a fourth floor."

"Maybe it's room two four zero."

"We don't have a room with that number either."

"Okay, it's definitely room four zero zero."

April gave up. The fucking moron didn't know where he belonged, and she lacked the patience or desire to deal with him while off the clock.

"How often does that happen?" Lane wanted to know.

"You'd be surprised. It's New Orleans, Baby."

She emotionally kept her distance with Lane—with everyone. But she never let go of him on the ten-minute walk to Decatur Street with her arm on his. Hope burned in his heart.

Discreetly, he watched April out the corner of his eye while they strolled through the Quarter. Oblivious to the beauty in the city because her magnificence distracted him.

When they stepped through the open-air entry of Café du Monde, a young couple in the back waved them over. Lane didn't recognize them at first. They both wore masquerade masks. When the woman's eyes locked with his, he knew who she was— he'd know Nicole's eyes anywhere.

Nicole stood to hug Lane, but Kovac pulled her back down before she could get close to him. "What gives?" she asked him defensively.

"Lane is a new vampire. Being his oldest and closest friend, your blood will be his greatest temptation."

"Oh," she conceded.

April and Lane knew what Kovac said didn't apply to

him, but they couldn't tell the two. It would mean sharing the prophecy with them.

April reassured Kovac, "Lane's already fed for the night, so no need to worry about him."

Chapter 43 ~ Kovac

Kovac again noticed April and Lane smelled similar. Discreetly, he sniffed their scents. They weren't just similar; they were identical.

The server brought them a plate of beignets and a café au lait each. Nicole and Lane simultaneously took a bite of their fried donut, covered in powdered sugar. Both choked on the sugar because they inhaled it with their bites. April or Kovac could have warned them first. Traditionally, locals found it more fun to let first timers figure out the proper way to eat beignets for themselves—never inhale when biting into a beignet.

Kovac rubbed Nicole's back while she coughed to catch her breath. April peered over her coffee at Lane, offering him no help. Over the sounds of the coughs, Kovac pinpointed the heartbeat of his best friend and her vampire. They beat as one. In his millennia, he'd heard nothing or smelled any two vampires like them. The mystery would nag at him until he solved it.

Only one theory could he conceive. Were they drinking from one another? That couldn't be it. Vampires can't survive without human blood.

The four of them spent most of their night together.

Kovac could count on one hand the number of times he'd seen joy on April's face. He always assumed she just didn't express happiness like everyone else. She tried to shake off her feelings as the night progressed, but failed miserably. He felt guilty not realizing his friend spent her nights unhappy. Maybe assuming her lack of joy for unhappiness was incorrect. She'd just never experienced bliss and contentment.

What kind of power did Lane have over his friend? He made her laugh. Kovac never heard April laugh. Would it last? Could he have even a taste of what he witnessed between the two with Nicole?

In between his observations, he listened to Nicole and Lane reminisce. Vampires leave their old lives and their pasts behind them. These two might never have to face that pain.

Could he really bring himself to do it? If she asked, would he deny her? She would just go running to Lane and beg him to turn her. Maybe he should just let him, and then he wouldn't have to carry the guilt. The thought of another vampire drinking his beautiful Nicole's blood turned his stomach over until it formed knots.

Why couldn't he live life as fearless as April? Even Nicole acted braver than him. She'd left everything she knew to explore the world while dying.

The couples parted ways when Nicole asked to go on a horse-drawn carriage ride. April may have found happiness, but romance—hell no—he could hear her say.

No longer occupied with the changes in his friend, he slipped his arm around Nicole to enjoy the romantic ride through the city. In all his years in New Orleans, he never found a reason to experience the historic activity.

Nicole snuggled up close to him. The feeling of her tucked up against his body convinced him he'd never get over losing her.

He felt damned if he cursed her and damned if he let her die.

At the hotel, he attempted the gentlemanly act of dropping her off with a kiss goodnight. Taking her into his arms for a brief, passionate kiss turned into a deeper need for one another.

She didn't protest when he scooped her up into his arms and carried her over the threshold of her room.

"Please, Kovac," she pleaded in between kisses while he laid her down on the bed. His heart ached, certain her pleas were for him to save her. Feigning ignorance, he took her please to mean "Make love to me."

She sat up to better position herself in order to pull his shirt over his head. Maybe her please did mean "Make love to me." A request Kovac had no problem granting.

He took his time, memorizing every inch of her body with his touch and then his eyes. What if she didn't ask him to make her a vampire? If she never asked him to turn her, he'd have every detail of her body imprinted in his head.

When he finished, she pushed him down to repeat the same motions. Watching her, studying every part of him. He felt at peace for the first time in his long life.

Boldly, as if being with him was her twentieth time and not her second, she slid herself down onto his ready body. She didn't move at first. She just enjoyed the feel of their bodies as one.

They made love 'till the sun came up. With Nicole sated and draped over his chest, he almost asked her what she wanted. "Nicole?" She'd fallen asleep before he could get the words out.

Chapter 44 ~ Nicole

Nicole left Kovac a note telling him she wanted some time with Lane and for him to come find her later in the city. She felt confident he could find her wherever she was.

She sent Lane a text asking him to meet her for dinner when he got up. After abandoning him, she felt rotten calling on him for advice like old times. Since he followed her, gave up mortality, and was not going anywhere, she might as well take advantage of the one person she could always count on.

Making her way to the French Market, she took her time checking out each vendor. She'd pictured a flea market, but found out just how wrong her imagination had been.

Flea markets are a fancy garage sale, whereas the French Market holds the essence of New Orleans' culture. The outdoor, open pavilion contained fruit and vegetable stands when she first walked in. Followed by snacks, treats, and the like unique to Louisiana.

One vendor sold only hot sauces. Popcorn sat in a bowl for people to use to sample each sauce. Nicole had never conceived such a wide variety of peppers and sauces existed. Tabasco, Crystal, and Frank's Hot Sauce were her limited knowledge regarding the subject.

She considered sitting at the counter to order a bowl of jambalaya but decided to hold off eating until she met up with Lane.

She purchased a bottle of Saint Charles Avenue Chardonnay for herself and a bottle of Bolden Vodka for Kovac. She almost got Lane a hat for his collection of baseball caps, but decided against it. All the choices would have made him look like a tourist.

Nicole, not being in any hurry, flipped through the artwork, memes, and sayings for sale. She found one she just had to buy for April. She might hate the glitter frame surrounding the funny statement, but she knew it was something April would say: *Seriously considering filling my pockets with glitter and whenever someone near me says something really stupid or rude, I'll just reach into my pocket with a dead expression and release the glitter into the sky above their head and watch it shower over them like a baptism of stupid.*

It was closing time, so Nicole grabbed the first bottle of hot sauce on her way out for Lane's gift, not wanting to leave him out of her present shopping.

The pizza place she stepped into on her stroll back toward Bourbon Street smelled like heaven. After finding a table, she sent Lane the address so he could find her.

The server dropped off the barbeque pizza she'd ordered just as Lane walked in. "Is it safe to hug you?" she asked him.

"You are always safe with me," her best friend assured her, bringing her in for an embrace. It felt good to be back in his arms like old times.

They both took their seats and dug into the pizza while it was hot. Nicole noticed Lane had different traits than her January. Where January would have immediately pushed her, knowing she wanted to talk, Lane patiently waited for her to say what she needed to say when she felt ready.

Putting off the main reason she requested he join her, she asked him instead, "Why Lane?"

Lane swallowed his food before answering her. "April told me beforehand I would have to choose a new name."

"Kovac told me that, too."

"What she didn't mention was how I would know what my name should be. I don't know if it happens this way for everyone. You know how they say your life flashes before your eyes when you're dying? Well, what I saw while I drank April's blood seemed like a vision of sorts. I saw a road. It felt like the road I traveled my mortal life on, and at the end of that road, I saw April waiting for me on the other side. Like the lane I journeyed down led me to her, where I always belonged. When she pulled her blood away and told me to choose my name, I just knew it was Lane."

"And you're not worried she will chew you up and spit you out when she's through with you?"

"The better question is—how long will it take her to face her new reality that she can't live without me?"

"I can see you are still as cocky as ever."

"Not as cocky. I'm cockier," he declared with a wink.

"Oh my, then we are all in trouble."

The server stopped by to see if they needed anything. Lane ordered another beer and asked for the cheque.

While picking at the remaining pieces of pizza left on her plate, Nicole finally voiced the reason she wanted to see him. "Kovac told me everything, but he hasn't officially offered to turn me. At least not in so many words."

"Remember, he has spent the last thousand years committed to keeping those he loved from this curse. You might have to just come out and tell him you want him to save you."

"What if he says no?" she whispered.

"Don't give him a choice. I'm sure you can find a way."

"What if I can't? Will you do it?"

"I can't," he said so quietly she barely heard him.

Looking up from her plate, the anger radiated from her eyes. "What do you mean, you can't?"

"Nikki, if you had asked me before I became a vampire, I would have done it without hesitation. I can't explain it, but it has to be Kovac who does it. Trust me." Regret filled his voice over denying her.

Enraged, she didn't want to hear anymore. She jumped up from the table, leaving behind her shopping bags and Lane —alone with his self-righteous attitude. She couldn't think straight, not understanding why the one person she always counted on told her he wouldn't save her.

Her feet couldn't carry her fast enough back to her room at the hotel.

Chapter 45 ~ April

She told Lane she'd reserved the room next to hers for him to stay in. The hurt in his eyes disappeared as quickly as it appeared. He grabbed his things and left her suite for the adjoining room.

April couldn't use the lumpy mattress excuse again. Loneliness was not a feeling she ever considered or paid any attention to. Trying to sleep a second night without Lane's presence made her painfully aware that being alone sucked. She did not know she'd been lying to herself all these centuries when she said being alone was her ideal dream. Lane exposed that lie for what it was—protection. Can't get hurt if you believe you are exactly as you want to be.

Her damn pride kept her from going to him. Two days without sleep, and still she refused to admit how much her heart wanted him. Even when he knocked on her door because he needed her blood.

"Nicole asked me to have dinner with her. Do you need my blood before I leave?" he considerately asked her. She craved his blood, but stupidly told him she'd be fine 'till later. Her throat burned with the need to feel his blood coating her glands. The taste still lingered on her tastebuds. It seemed they smelled identical, but in reality, the cloves were her scent and the cinnamon belonged to him. The combination of two scents merged into one.

She sulked in her room for a while after he left. April had to get out of her head. The guaranteed cure for her angst sat in her garden.

The second she stepped out of her suite, the emergency lights and sirens went off. This week appeared to have the goal of making the history books. Their emergency lights and sirens were to only get activated because of an out-of-control vampire. Like the banks' silent alarm, this alarm sent a direct call to the hunters. Since moving back to New Orleans, the need to trigger the alarm hadn't arisen.

Running down the stairs to assess the situation, she ran into Kovac on his way to do the same thing.

They could smell the blood from the top of the first flight of stairs.

A male rogue vampire had Nelly by the throat. They were too late to save her. He'd nearly drained her dry based on the color of her skin.

April's and Kovac's fangs elongated in defense, along with their claws that only appeared when they needed to protect themselves. Both crouched down in a fighting stance, ready to attack.

All the guests in their rooms were safe. When the alarm went off, all the rooms' hidden automatic locks triggered, locking the residents inside for their safety. The phone systems shut down and a cell phone jammer clicked on. They didn't need humans calling 911 in a panic. Just a few of the many safety precautions set in place to protect the humans.

The unknown immortal threw Nelly's body across the room when he saw Kovac and April. Eyes still blood red. He'd been gorging on blood for so long that Nelly's blood didn't satisfy his lust.

Nelly's blood dripped from his fangs. Based on the amount of blood smeared across his face and covering his hands, he'd ripped her throat open to consume every drop.

Standing with bent knees and hands out by his side in an I-dare-you-to-come-get-me mode, "Where is she?" he demanded.

"Where is who?" Kovac calmly asked. April knew he seethed inside, but kept himself in check to avoid escalating the attacker.

"Cinder!" Spit mixed with blood flew out of his mouth. "I can still smell her here. What did you do with her?"

The front door pushed open before either could come up with an excuse for the disappearance of Cinder. A tear-soaked Nicole walked straight into the wrath of the thirsty vampire.

He took advantage, thinking a human hostage would get him the answers he desperately sought. Pulling Nicole around to the front of his chest to use her like a shield. He wrapped his claws around her neck to secure her to his body. His teeth pricked her neck before they could react, while his hand wrapped around her throat. He licked her blood that trickled from the wounds.

Lane burst through the doors—carrying Nicole's shopping bags—in chase of her. At the same time, the vampire moaned with sickening pleasure. Clearly, enjoying the taste of Nicole's blood mixed with her fear.

Lane's instinct to protect those he loved made him drop the items in his hand to move recklessly to her defense. "Lane, don't!" April shouted at him.

The vampire looking for Cinder turned slightly in Lane's

direction. Nicole winced with the movement. "Yes, Lane, listen to your friends. One move and I snap her neck." His claws pressed deeper into her open wounds.

Curiosity appeared on the vamp's face. Nicole cringed when he brought his nose to her and inhaled deeply. "Now, that's interesting. This human smells like all three of you. She must be very important to you. I wonder which one of you she means the most to?" His words came out in a hiss through his fangs.

The three's anger was on full display. Their fangs dripped with venom in anticipation of the moment they could overpower the immortal who would threaten Nicole. The deep breaths they took to maintain their self-control barely held them in place.

"Tsk. Tsk. I'd calm down if I were you guys. All you need to do is tell me where to find Cinder, and you can have your preciousss human."

With the need to stall until Bobby showed up, Kovac asked him, "Tell me your name, and I can look in our logs to see if she left you any messages."

The fucking moron bought Kovac's idiotic suggestion. April resisted the urge to laugh at him.

"Spenser. But I warn you, you'd better not try anything."

Kovac pretended to search the books, while Lane and April remained rooted to their spots. For humans, the hunters moved with the speed of an immortal when they busted in through the front doors. Their tasers hit Spenser before he could move.

His body pulsed violently from the electric shock. His claws were still wrapped around Nicole's neck when he fell forward to the floor, taking Nicole down with him.

Chapter 46 ~ Kovac

Kovac raced his body faster than he'd ever moved toward Nicole to catch her. It wasn't fast enough. His terror filled screams shook the room. He tossed Spenser's body toward Bobby and his men.

Pulling Nicole into his lap, he checked for her pulse. He found it, but it was faint.

"Turn her," Lane demanded.

Kovac's voice, laced with agony, admitted, "I don't know if it's what she wants. I can't do it without her permission."

"She asked me to change her at dinner. It's her will," Lane assured him.

"Then you do it," Kovac begged.

"It has to be you, Kovac," April told him.

Kovac searched his friend's eyes, begging for her help. "Look at us. Her blood is only calling you." Kovac looked back and forth between April and Lane. Both of their fangs had retracted once Spenser had been subdued. His fangs still hung low, begging to do what they were meant for.

The tears pooled down the sides of his face. He again

asked, "What if this isn't what she wants?"

"Which possibility is least desirable? The fate of oblivion or the fate of immortality without her? Take a chance, Kovac. Do this for both of you," April told her mentor and dearest friend.

With her pulse weakening by the second, Kovac was out of time. He bent down to taste the sweet blood of his beautiful Nicole, then he bit into his wrist. Lane held Nicole's mouth open so Kovac wouldn't have to set her down. The droplets of blood needed for the exchange he offered her slid down her throat.

He removed his wrist and sealed his wound with his saliva. The three waited. Time stood still, watching Nicole's body.

Kovac hadn't vanished from existence, giving him hope they would both be all right.

His heart beat again when her body began shaking out of control. Being unconscious kept her from screaming through the pain. Her mortal blood seeped from her pores until her veins filled with the blood of immortals.

The most beautiful vampire the world would ever know opened her eyes, now nearly black like his. Full of joy, he held her tight against his body.

For the first time, he didn't feel the heaviness of his curse. Holding Nicole, he felt a peace he'd thought impossible.

Gently, she pushed away from him. "Ruby, is the name I choose to spend eternity with—with you by my side."

Chapter 47 ~ Lane

Kovac and Ruby went to his suite to clean her up. When Kovac gave her a moment to embrace her friend before they left, he whispered to her, "If you feel a desire to drink from Kovac, don't fight it."

Ruby searched his eyes to discern her friend's sincerity.

"Trust me." He used his persuasive voice, almost calling her Nikki because she would have fully trusted him then. They would need a new code name.

Lane and April assisted the hunters with the aftermath Spencer's rampage left behind.

A crime scene cleaning crew removed all evidence of the tragedy in record time. Nelly's corpse was placed in a body bag and brought to the morgue—presumably with no family to notify.

Roger, who'd hid under the counter after pressing the alarm they had trained him to push if anything paranormal occurred during one of his shifts, went with Bobby. But not before letting April know he quit while he shredded his work and business cards in defiance. The hunters had procedures for dealing with the trauma he suffered.

Lane agreed to go door to door, letting those locked inside out of their rooms. April took half, and he took the other half.

They issued apologies, brought water bottles to each room, and let them all know the bar was open if they needed a drink.

The explanation they'd been given: "We had a system malfunction with the doors and phones. The electric company fixed it as quicky as they could."

"Why would these doors have hidden locks on them to begin with?" they asked.

"For whatever reason, the original owners installed them during the reconstruction." The facts they left out were that the original owners still lived and precautions had to remain for the safety of everyone.

The vampires who got stuck locked in their rooms, some of them just went out the windows for the night. They granted those who waited around the truth.

Lane left April on her own after he finished letting out the last person assigned to him. The sun rose on the horizon when Lane went to his room. He wouldn't beg. He'd take whatever April felt comfortable giving him. Then, when she let go of all her defenses, he'd be whatever she needed him to be.

After his shower, he lay down again by himself.

The sun had barely set when the door of his room squeaked open, waking him from his slumber. The direction of the noise came from the adjoining suite, April's suite. Lane didn't move at first.

Both stubbornly waited on the other to make a move. Lane in his bed. April with her back to the door separating the two rooms.

Lane caved first. Sitting up in the bed, what he saw broke him. April held in the tears she refused to let fall. Eyes crimson red, in desperate need of his blood.

"You are one stubborn hellcat," Lane softly told her. Staring at her with his bedroom eyes, he tempted her with all he could give her.

April closed her eyes and sucked in the air surrounding her. "Why do you have to be so damn sexy?" she asked while obviously trying to avoid noticing his exposed chest, the just woke up erection, or his bare feet sticking out from under the white sheet.

He didn't have an answer to her question. When she couldn't resist looking at him for a moment longer, he winked in her direction. Barely resisting the intoxication of her arousal, Lane obstinately remained where he sat.

"I don't want romance," she told him.

"You told me that already," he reminded her.

"I don't cuddle or hold hands."

"What else?" he encouraged her to keep going.

"I'll never say the L word."

"Keep going." Lane winked again. He then threw the sheet off, revealing he slept in the nude.

April gulped at the sight of his perfect body. "I don't make love."

"Anything else?" he asked as he moved to the edge of the bed.

"I liked it when you called me Hellcat."

"Take what you need, my Hellcat." Lane turned his neck, inviting her to make the next move.

In the blink of an eye, she'd pierced his vein to quench the thirst only he could douse.

Chapter 48 ~ Ruby

Ruby walked up the three flights of stairs under Kovac's arm. Unsure how to express the joy she felt. Death no longer called her name. And Kovac turned her himself.

He brought her to his suite and started the shower for her. Her clothes ruined from the blood—her blood. Kovac helped her out of them.

She stepped into the shower. Turning to him, she invited him in. "Join me?"

Kovac removed his clothes to grant her request. Standing in front of the woman he sired—the woman he loved—the water mixed with blood poured down her beautiful body.

He reached up with the tips of his fingers to push the hair out of her eyes. "Kiss me," she begged, while looking into his eyes.

If he couldn't deny her immortality, he would never deny her anything. With his lips on hers, she wrapped her arms around his neck. Picking her up into his arms, he placed her against the shower wall and then set her down on his length.

With their bodies joined as one, Ruby's fangs busted

through her gums for the first time, in need of blood—Kovac's blood. Remembering Lane's advice, she didn't ask permission when instinct told her how to fulfill her desire.

Kovac's body tensed momentarily when she punctured his neck. He tasted of vanilla and honeysuckle, her two favorite scents. She took only what she needed before closing the wound.

When she unashamedly looked into Kovac's now red eyes, she smiled at him and yielded her neck to him. Even though he acted leery of his sudden need for her blood, he didn't resist taking what he wanted.

With their need for blood satiated, he pumped in and out of her until her inner walls squeezed him, pulling everything from inside of him into her.

He still had her pressed up against the tiles when she asked, "Help me clean up?"

Gently, he set her down to accommodate her wishes. Spoiling her for eternity was all he wanted to do. Kovac reached around Ruby's back for the shampoo. He poured more than necessary into the palm of his hand and scrubbed every drop of blood from her hair.

Ruby's eyes found his. Eyes she wanted to gaze into for all of eternity. "I love you, my beautiful Ruby."

"I love you, too, Kovac. To Pluto and back." Forgetting about finishing the shower, he scooped her up and carried her to the bed to make love again to his eternal companion.

First, he asked her, "Why Pluto?"

"Because the moon isn't far enough to express how much I love you."

Chapter 49 ~ Kovac

Kovac woke with Ruby sitting on his chest, fangs out, ready for blood. Not understanding why his blood called to her but unwilling to say no—he submitted to her.

After another passionate round of lovemaking with Ruby in the shower, Kovac texted April to meet them. Maybe she had some answers, because he now knew for certain she and Lane were drinking from each other as well.

She told them to meet her and Lane in the garden.

When they arrived in the courtyard, Kovac pulled a chair out for Ruby and then sat down next to her. Curious, watching April's birds as they stood on Lane as if he was her, Kovac felt unsure which question to ask first.

Lane broke the ice. "Ruby, did you take my advice?"

Ruby nodded, her cheeks flushed in embarrassment.

"What advice?" Kovac asked.

"I told her, if your blood called to her, not to resist it."

"What do you two know?" Kovac probed further.

April stood up in her t-shirt, *Seriously, I don't know exactly when the UFO dumped off all of these stupid people. But apparently, they aren't coming back for them,* and got too close for comfort to compare Kovac and Ruby's scent.

Slightly aggravated, he asked his friend, "Did you find out what you needed to know?"

"I have to confirm some things before I tell you what Bobby told the two of us."

"Bobby Faciane, the hunter? What does he have to do with anything?"

"I had questions, too. I took a chance the other night that he might have answers."

"Go on."

"I know Ruby drank your blood. Did you drink hers?"

"Yes."

"What did she taste like?"

"That's a little personal, don't you think?"

"I'm going somewhere with my questions. I promise. I'd bet money she tastes different from any human you ever drank from and you taste just like her. If you don't want to tell me exactly what she tastes like, go compare notes and come back. If it's the same, that's all you need to tell me."

Kovac and Ruby stepped away. "Do you want to go at the same time?" Ruby suggested.

With his fingers Kovac counted, one, two, three. "Honeysuckle and vanilla," they admitted in unison. Both of their eyes popped open in surprise.

Before going back to the two waiting for them, he leaned in for a purposeful sniff of her. "Why is everyone smelling me? Do I stink?" Ruby asked him.

He chuckled, "No. I noticed Lane and April smelled exactly the same, and I assume April checked to see if we share the same quality."

"Do we?" she asked, while trying to figure it out for herself.

"I believe so."

"How? Why?"

"I'm hoping April knows." Kovac grabbed her hand and together they walked back. He sat down first and pulled Ruby onto his lap. Whatever information April had for them, he wanted Ruby as close to him as possible.

"Tell us what you know," Kovac practically demanded.

"Patience, my old friend. I have one more question. Have you noticed anything about Ruby's heartbeat?"

"I'll appease you, but this better be the last question. I'm anxious to know what you know."

Focused on her heartbeat, it only took a moment to realize it beat in sync with his. Perplexed, he tuned into April's and Lane's hearts, confirming their hearts still beat as one, just as he'd noticed when they sat in Café du Monde.

Ruby placed a hand over his heart and the other over hers to feel their indistinguishable rhythmic beat. "That's so beautiful," she told him.

They both looked back at April for the explanation.

"We noticed the same similarities after I turned Lane into a vampire. I even took Lane out to see if he could drink human blood, which he couldn't. Anger and jealously rose inside of me when he tried. He encouraged me to see if I could still drink human blood. Lane went into a nearly uncontrollable rage when I tried. I failed. If I hadn't, he may have killed the human.

"We told Bobby our story. He told us there is a prophecy they have always brushed off as myth."

April closed her eyes to use her near perfect memory to quote the prophecy. "Even in damnation there is mercy. My children will never rest in my bosom. They will never look upon my face. Fear keeps them from me. But I will not forget them. Vampires who prove their worthiness by refraining from killing will one day find their equal. They will know their equal by the identical beat of their hearts, by the matching taste of blood, and by the satisfaction of the blood that only their equal can provide. The blood of innocents can no longer quench their thirst. Man was never meant to be alone. Lucifer tricked them into choosing a life apart from me. But that doesn't mean I will ever forget them and their needs. This gift cannot be forced or sought after. An equal is only found by one worthy and should not be pursued."

Kovac sat, shocked. The only dream he ever desired sat in his lap. Ruby was, without a doubt, his equal. A gift to him. Mercy he didn't deserve—he held in his arms.

His shock turned to laughter. He laughed so hard he had to move Ruby so he could stand up.

April brazenly asked him, "I don't get it. What's so funny?"

It took some effort on his part to calm himself so he could talk. "I'm laughing at you."

"What do you mean?"

"Well, the one person who wanted to spend eternity alone has an eternal companion, an equal. The irony is hilarious." His composure improved enough to allow his feelings to express concern. "How are you handling it?"

"We are figuring it out," is the only thing his friend had to say about the matter. However, the look in her eyes spoke volumes. She might never admit it, but she was madly in love with Lane.

Epilogue ~ April

April stood with Lane—wearing the only shirt she owned without a smartass comment on it—behind their best friends as they publicly committed their lives to each other. Marriage licenses weren't possible, since Kovac didn't legally exist. Still, Ruby felt the need for a ceremony.

April didn't understand the sentiment and said as much to Lane. "We're never doing this."

He didn't argue with her.

Having him by her side all the time hadn't been as terrible as she'd imagined. He allowed her to be who she was without complaint or suggestions on how to improve herself. She assumed any man would demand she brought what most saw as flaws to heel.

Lane's treatment of her was based on the corny philosophy, "Be yourself. Because who you are is good." She even told him he sounded dorky and his response was, "I'm trying to sound smart here. Back me up, would you?"

As eye-rolling as his attitude was, it was the most loving thing he could do for her.

If she wasn't true to herself, Lane wouldn't love her the way he did. Yeah, she knew he loved her, but he respected her wish to not talk about it. The look in his eyes for her was like a mirror she couldn't avoid.

He even agreed without hesitation to leave Kovac and Ruby to discover themselves on their own. The couple would stay in New Orleans for a few more years, while she and Lane were leaving the next evening for the New York hotel.

They would set everything up with the new employees and establish themselves as the "new ownership." Lane suggested keeping the current management on, so they could take lots of vacations to travel like she wanted to.

Having seen much of the world meant nothing, as it was forever changing. Her world sure did change when January Taylor—now Lane—walked through the doors of Hotel Lamia.

The lesson she learned: maybe she didn't know everything.

Join April and Lane in New York next time in
Hotel Lamia, New York: Where Immortals Sleep

From the Author

Thank you for falling in love with my characters. When you read my words, they come alive even more so for me. I write what I want to read, and I create individuals I'd like to hang out with. I believe in happily ever after, and happily throughout. Not that I don't read novels full of constant pain, drama, and suspense, but I'd much rather read something that puts a smile on my face from beginning to end. That's what I hope you experience when you read my books.

This journey is only just beginning for me, and I hope you stick around through it all.

This particular book holds an extra special place in my heart. The April character's personality I built from three individuals who mean the world to me. They aren't entirely April, but much of her comes from them.

The memes and quotes on April's t-shirts were taken from the group text messages my hotel friends and I still send to each other regularly.

Book five, in my *Soulmate Call* series, is my next project. It takes place right after Hurricane Katrina. The aftermath sends all the characters into one home as they rebuild and recover. Scott and Kelly Lockhart are on the verge of splitting up, as Kelly feels neglected and longs for more out of her marriage. In a house full of individuals, with telepathic capabilities, it's only a matter of time before the Lockhart's discover the secret and rekindle their love as true soulmates.

The audio version of book one and two in the series is available on Audible or on my podcast, *The Soulmate Call Series*, wherever you listen to your podcast. Three and four still to come.

If you are an author, I love supporting others. Look me up. I prefer romance reads, especially with a fantasy, sci-fi, or paranormal twist.

Reviews on Amazon, Goodreads, and Facebook are an author's bread and butter. Thank you.

If you don't already please like, follow, invite your friends, and share my pages.
https://facebook.com/tiffanyannbooks

https://instagram.com/tiffanyann_books
https://twitter.com/tiffanyannbooks
https://goodreads.com/tiffanyann_books

For a sample of my debut novel, *The Soulmate Call,* flip to the end.

Coming Soon
The Soulmate Call Series

The Soulmate Rekindled – Scott's & Kelly's story

The Soulmate Dilemma- Samuel's & Samantha's story

The Soulmate Homecoming- Sarah's & Benjamin's story

The Soulmate Beginning – Ezekiel's & Annabelle's story

The Soulmate Triangle – Caleb's & Avery's story

The Soulmate Reunion – Meg's & Jack's story

Previous Works

The Soulmate Call- Rey's & Lisabeth's story

The Soulmate Battle – Caleb's & Pasiphae's story

The Soulmate Restoration – Luke's & Danielle's story

The Soulmate Healing – Cole's & Darion's story

Upcoming Projects

Love Letters from the Edge of the World -
loosely based on a true story

The Book of Judges series- a historical fiction series based
on the love of the Father as seen through the eyes of Judges

The Soulmate Call

Prologue-Lisabeth

I once watched a girl bite into almost every piece of chocolate in a heart-shaped box of chocolates. She would take a bite and put the chocolate back. I wondered why she did that with the chocolate.

Before I could ask her, she told me why, "Each one of us is like a piece of chocolate. Some guy comes along, and you give your heart to him. If he isn't the right guy, it's like he figuratively took a bite out of your heart before giving it back to you. All the pieces of chocolate with a bite in them are what your heart looks like when you have given it away more than once, only to get it back broken. The pieces of chocolate with bites taken out of them can't become whole again because the bite damages the pieces of chocolate. Giving your heart to someone who is unworthy is giving a piece of yourself away—you can never get back."

That example stuck with me. Her analogy caused my reasoning behind why I always chose the type of guy I knew couldn't break my heart.

Anyone would describe me as absolutely and completely selfish in my approach to picking boys. Selfish, meaning I wanted to enjoy life, but my heart I kept for one person and one person only. I would find a guy who had a girlfriend already, or a guy not worth giving your heart to, or one whom I knew my parents wouldn't approve of.

Besides being selfish and not wanting a broken heart, I knew *Mr. Right* had to be worthy of my parents' approval. I wanted to have fun without commitment, but when I, Lisabeth Gilbert, settled down, I wanted my parents' blessing.

When you're only looking for fun, you keep your heart guarded and surround it with six-inch steel walls. I'd yet to find a guy around worthy of giving my heart to.

The guy with a girlfriend, he obviously wasn't looking for a commitment, and since he cheated on his girlfriend, he definitely didn't qualify giving your heart to. The one who mirrored me, wanting to have fun, and not bring home to your parents' worthy, also wasn't looking to commit. If any one of them started acting like they were thinking about something serious, I would end that relationship faster than it began.

Jeffrey Turner fit my only fun, no strings attached criteria. He had a girlfriend when we met. Instantly, I identified him as a total player. Only looking for a good time as well. He started off our friendship by flirting with me. It didn't hurt he was good at it, too. I also labeled him as the most gorgeous player I had ever met. Six feet tall, chocolate brown eyes (my biggest weakness), deep dimples (the kind that made an appearance with every movement of his mouth), a chiseled body, chestnut hair he kept cut military style, and lips that tasted delicious just by looking at them.

We'd met at Lonestar steakhouse where I waited tables when I turned seventeen. I came into work one day, and all the girls were talking about the new guy and how hot he looked. He had recently moved from Texas to be near his girlfriend, who also worked at the restaurant. He had moved in with his grams and enrolled in the same community college I planned on attending in the fall.

We quickly became friends. We flirted and sought each other out at work every day. He'd call me on the phone to tell me about all his conquests back home, and I bragged about mine. Convincing a guy to agree to hook up with you when you straight up told him you wanted to have fun and didn't want a boyfriend proved easy.

When I said hook-up, I'm not talking about sex. I'm definitely not that kind of player. I'm no innocent girl either, but I drew the line at intercourse. I wanted to make out and go only as far as one could without doing the deed. I had my reasons.

We ended up in biology together at school. Rey—was what everyone called him, not Jeff but Rey—how sexy is that? We flirted while making plans to hook up for a couple of months. The girlfriend always impeded us from ever actually getting together for fun. Fine by me because I enjoyed the flirting, and neither of us moved toward making a commitment or getting hurt.

We finally got in one date, a sort of lunch date, at one of those *hole-in-the-wall* Chinese restaurants. We went looking for a place to park afterward, but his truck broke down. What were the chances?

A couple of weeks later, he called me up to ask me to come over to his place. Of course, everything cute I owned had to be dirty that day. I threw on a pair of jeans and my favorite t-shirt of the singer Plumb that I'd found on my floor, with my platform flip-flops, and headed out the door.

We spent the next hour or two doing what horny teenagers do. We had fun making out, except he had a no kissing rule.

Remember when I said he had lips that tasted delicious just by looking at them? Then, I found out I couldn't kiss them. Argh! Well, I had rules, so how could I argue with his rules? He made up the lamest excuse, though. "He wasn't cheating on his girlfriend if he didn't kiss me." My eyes were rolling in my mind at that line. Whatever; all I heard in his reason, he didn't want to kiss me.

When we finished, he had tears in his eyes. A strange sight for me to see a guy crying after we had been fooling around. He said he felt guilty, and he realized he loved his girlfriend. I couldn't fault him for that. I actually believed him. I stood there holding him while he sobbed. He made me promise to keep our afternoon to myself, so I did.

The next day, I walked through the parking lot at school to go to class, when he came racing up next to me in his bright two-toned green pickup truck. When he rolled his window down, I could tell something had him angry. He practically yelled at me, "Get in!" Confused, I opened the door and climbed in.

He accused me of telling some guy in one of my classes about us. The accusation was so strange. The scene played out so fast, I didn't even know how to defend myself. I denied everything, but he didn't even hear me. The next words out of his mouth were, "Get out! I never want to see you again."

That day I remember as the most confusing day of my life. I respected his wishes and left him alone. That next semester, we had no classes together, and he had quit working at the steakhouse. Having gone our separate ways, we never ran into each other anymore.

He didn't break my heart the way a lover would, but we had become good friends over those few months. I missed our friendship. Not being one to hang onto those kinds of things, I moved on to the next guy that same day.

I thought about him occasionally and wondered what happened. Maybe I would never know. It haunted me knowing I would never know what those delicious lips feel or taste like.

Lisabeth - July 10, 1999

&

The morning drive to orientation went at a snail's pace with all the traffic on the interstate. The drive into New Orleans early in the morning was easily always a capital B. I dreaded spending my whole Saturday listening to lectures about how great UNO is.

For the first year of college, I went to the local community college, and now I had to move on to a university if I wanted my degree. On a Saturday morning, being a young 18-year-old, I would've rather slept on my day off.

I pulled up to the campus in search of a place to park; I had absolutely no idea where to go, having never been there before. I should have probably checked the place out before today. At least I left early enough to guarantee I wouldn't be late. I hated being tardy.

After finding a parking space, the time had arrived to go search for the auditorium where I planned on spending the next few hours listening to some speech about how the future was bright. I half expected to hear some lame slogan like, *the future's so bright, you'll need sunglasses.*

Why didn't I see if anybody I knew planned on going to this thing? When I got closer to the building, I saw someone I knew. I felt relief wash all over me, thinking, *Maybe this day won't be that bad?* Seeing my friend Daniel eased some of the tension.

I couldn't even remember how, where, or when we met. He always seemed to be wherever I went, whether it was at the coffee shop I liked to hang out at or with a group of friends. And there he stood, waiting for orientation to start. He was one of those guys I could bring home to my parents, so I'd purposely always kept him at a distance. He was also not the most attractive guy either. He wasn't ugly, but for some unexplainable reason, he never did it for me at all. We were close to the same height, which could have been worse. He could have been shorter than me. Looks wise, in my mind, he was plain old average—average hair, average eyes, average size—blah.

I felt saved, though, knowing I wouldn't have to sit all by myself through the long day. We walked into the auditorium, having the usual casual talk two people experience when they are mere acquaintances and not great friends.

I walked through the auditorium doors with Daniel. I paused because sitting in the back row with his body turned around in his seat, looking at something outside of the doors, sat Rey. Then he moved toward me, and my brown eyes met his brown eyes. I was suddenly hit with a giant tidal wave of feelings. A wave of emotions I had never felt before. If Cupid really shot people in the butt with arrows, they hit mine. It felt a lot like love at first sight, or should I say love at first re-sight. It felt possibly like my soul took over by taking a sledgehammer and utterly destroying any wall or barrier I had ever built around my heart. Out of nowhere, the first thought in my head surprised me. *"I love you, Jeffrey Turner."*

Rey never took his eyes off of mine. His gaze was so intense I could feel it. I knew I didn't see him open his mouth to speak, yet I knew with every fiber of my very being I heard him say, *"I love you too, Lisabeth Gilbert."*

Impossible, or crazy, came to visit me. I heard him say it in my mind. So shaken up, I nearly tripped going down the stairs while my mind spun. Rey jumped up to grab me by the elbow, and he pulled me close to him. While still looking me straight in the eyes, I heard in my head, *"You're not crazy."* This time, he opened his mouth and asked, "Can we go outside and talk?"

The only words I could find to mumble out of my mouth were, "Give me a minute."

I strolled to a seat with Daniel to set my stuff down. Daniel must have seen something going on. "Are you all right? You're white as a sheet. You look like you might vomit or something?"

I paused and turned to him, my thoughts all over the place. I didn't even answer him. All I could think about revolved around that first thought I had. *"I love you, Jeffrey Turner?"* Where did that come from? When did I fall in love with him? How come I just realized this? What was going on? These questions ran through my mind. Never mind the fact I heard his voice in my head, not once, but twice. Never mind, he loved me, too.

I thought Daniel may have been right, I might vomit. Without even answering him, I got up and headed out the door. I didn't know where I was going, but I had to get out of there. The walls closing in on me, my chest getting heavier. I moved faster to get outside.

Rey

Stuck sitting in the back row at the stupid orientation my friends dragged me to. I hadn't been myself for months. I only left my house out of necessity. I hadn't been up to moving on with my life, pretending nothing ever happened. My friends wore me down. They wouldn't stop nagging me.

They meant well, but they didn't understand how stupid I'd acted. How I'd ruined the best thing that ever happened to me. How I'd pushed her away, and she didn't know why. How tortured I felt, knowing I would probably never see her again. How she was my happiness; I ran away because it scared me. I wasn't ready. Once I accepted who we were to each other, I didn't know how to find her.

I sat there, in the back row in the stadium, doomed to spend a miserable day, when I suddenly somehow felt her presence, certain she'd arrived there somewhere. Terrified to look around for her to find out my feelings were wrong, but also scared to not search and miss her. I didn't hesitate for another second; I turned around and quickly began scanning through the mass of people for her.

I found her. Lisabeth really had registered for the orientation, too. I couldn't believe my eyes. Was I really seeing her, or was I dreaming? If it were a dream, I hoped I wouldn't wake up from it.

She saw me, too. Our eyes met. I refused to look away. I may have felt ashamed of how I'd treated her, but I wouldn't take my eyes off of her ever again. If she allowed me to look into her beautiful brown eyes forever, I would.

Proud of myself for remembering the color of her eyes. Most days I believed her eyes were every bit as brown as mine were, but some days I doubted my memory. There were days when my depression became so intense, I convinced myself I might have forgotten what she looked like, but I hadn't. How could I forget? She looked exactly the way I remembered her, and more.

While those thoughts ran through my mind, I heard her. I heard her in my head. She called to my soul, *"I love you, Jeffrey Turner."*

My heart stopped. Before taking another breath, I spoke back into her thoughts, into her soul, *"I love you too, Lisabeth Gilbert."* I knew this would probably terrify her, but she had to know I heard her. Desperate for her. I couldn't lose her again, even if it meant scaring her at first.

She tripped on the stadium stairs. I jumped to my feet to catch her. I pulled her close, never taking my eyes off of hers. Not wasting a second to drink in her smell while enjoying the feel of her body so close to mine.

I heard her saying she must be crazy, so I pushed my thoughts toward hers, reassuring her, *"You're not crazy."* I used my voice to ask her to join me outside. It's clear she seemed in some sort of shock because she asked me for a minute.

I continued to keep my eyes fixed on her, afraid if I looked away, she would disappear.

My friends noticed me smiling for the first time in months, causing their questions to come at me like speeding bullets. Without looking away from her, I told them, "It's her; she's the one, my Lisabeth."

She slowly headed out the door. I moved to follow her, her pace quickening. I knew I scared her, but I could only hope she would get over it. Once she understood who we were to each other, she would forgive me. I prayed.

She looked too adorable, pacing back and forth. When she started having trouble breathing, appearing to be having a panic attack or something, I immediately rushed over to her and gently pulled her to me. She let me hold her in my arms. She even rested her head on my chest. Lisabeth fit in my arms so perfectly.

I felt her body shaking, her heart pounding, and I felt lost, with no idea how to help her. Clueless about the hows of loving someone or taking care of them. Just one of the many reasons I ran away. I held her for a while before I even said anything. She slowly calmed down. When I felt her stop shaking, it gave me some comfort, hoping I did something right.

She looked up at me with her gorgeous eyes, making me want to tell her everything. However, I knew I needed to start slow, or I risked scaring her away. I struggled to know where to even begin. *"Yes, Lisabeth, you can hear my thoughts inside your mind. I heard your voice in my head and you can hear mine in yours."* I saw the confusion clearly all over her face.

Then I heard her say, *"But how?"*

"It's a long story. I want to explain everything to you, but there isn't time for me to explain it to you how you deserve. The orientation is going to start. I don't want to skip anything I have to tell you. Will you eat lunch with me? I will start by telling you all I can get in during that time. I will tell you this. I know what is going on and why. I need to ask you to trust me and to give me a chance." I said all of this through our thoughts because I wanted her to get used to hearing my voice inside of her.

When she nodded her head, I continued with my voice. "I have to first tell you how sorry I'm for the way I treated you that day. I acted like a scared idiot. I feared how I felt about you. I made the whole thing up. I needed you mad at me. I didn't know how else to justify running away from you. Please forgive me."

I held my breath, waiting for her to respond. She surprised me by responding in our thoughts. *"Of course, I forgive you. I never held it against you. I understood something happened, and you did what you felt you had to do."*

When her words poured into my mind, it felt like she somehow made me whole from the inside out. She completed me when she opened herself up to me and gave herself over to who we were. We were soulmates. She was the other half of my soul. Our souls had sought each other and had found each other.

I took her hand in mine to walk back inside. I felt I must tell her one thing, "Lisabeth, I will explain everything, but the one thing I want to mention right now is we can only hear each other if we're looking at each other. If you turn away from me, I can't hear you and vice versa. It has something to do with our eyes being the window to our souls. I know that probably doesn't make much sense to you. It will after I tell you all about it. I didn't want you to say something and I miss it. I know that would probably confuse you more than you are already. I meant it earlier; I really do love you. I have loved you ever since I first laid eyes on you. Only problem, I gave into my fear of commitment, ignoring the feelings I had for you. I know—I'm overwhelming you, so I'm going to shut up now."

She stopped walking to look up at me. *"I'm overwhelmed, scared, and confused. I don't understand it and I definitely can't explain it, but I choose to trust you. That is all that matters at this moment. Right now, I like I don't have to be vulnerable out loud. I don't think I could be. I have never been vulnerable with—anyone.*

It's quite scary. We will both have to be patient with each other." Without even waiting for me to respond, she turned back and started walking inside.

Lisabeth

Rey headed back toward his friends, and I returned to my seat with Daniel. My mind went into overdrive. I had absolutely no idea how I might get anything out of the presentation. I couldn't imagine what Daniel might have been thinking, and I guess if I spoke honestly, I really didn't care.

I somehow could hear someone's thoughts, and he could hear mine. As a huge *Star Trek* fan, I found this to be mind blowingly exceptional. As a regular human who believed all things like telepathy to be science fiction, I still found it to be mind blowingly exceptional.

Also, terrifying. We both barely knew each other, and now we both were supposedly in love. Not even sure I knew what love felt like. What if we didn't actually like each other? Were we now stuck with one another? I had so many questions, so many fears, and so much excitement all at the same time. How might I even process what happened? Between discovering my genuine feelings and being connected to someone in such a way, we could hear each other's thoughts seemed more than any one person should have to process at a time. Were we the only two people in the world like this? Rey said he knew what happened, so he must know other people who could do this.

Lost in my thoughts, I had forgotten Daniel sat next to me until he shoved my shoulder. "Hey, Lisabeth, are you here? I have been saying your name."

I looked over at him with a blank stare. Apologizing seemed the most logical course. Not like I could explain what happened. I would've gotten escorted to the looney bin where they would've locked me up and thrown away the key. After a moment, I told him what I could. "I'm sorry, Daniel. I saw someone I used to hang out with. I realized he meant more to me than a casual friend. It's a bit of a shock to me. I'm trying to process my feelings. I went outside, and he followed me. I found out he feels the same way, and he has been looking for me. It's all so sudden and unexpected. I'm not even sure where to go from here."

I stumbled over my poorly executed explanation when Rey unexpectedly plopped down in the seat next to me. Then he reached across me to introduce himself to Daniel. I knew they were talking, but my brain acted so overloaded all I heard were sounds. I literally shook my head, trying to clear the fog. I then turned my head to look at Rey, since he told me I had to look at him to talk into his thoughts. *"What are you doing? You look like a jealous boyfriend."*

He smiled at me, in a way that made me think if I were standing, I would feel weak in the knees. *"Maybe I'm a jealous boyfriend."*

"Oh, so you're my boyfriend now? When did that happen?"

"I know it's not official yet, but it will be soon enough."

"Confident, are you?"

"You haven't told me to shove off, so yes, I feel pretty confident. Do you mind if I sit with you? I could sit back there, but all I would do is stare at the back of your head the whole time. I figured, this way, maybe I would hear something the administration said today." We both went back and forth with one another. He made an excellent point. All I would've done all day would include resisting the urge to turn around to look at him the whole time.

"Did you forget I can hear you?" Rey sarcastically asked me, making my face turn three different shades of red. *"I guess it's*

safe to say I can sit here," he told me confidently, and followed it with a wink.

Argh, *"He is going to be the death of me,"* I said to myself, this time remembering to turn my head so he couldn't hear me.

I barely made it through those last couple of hours. Rey's knee pressed up against my knee the whole time. I couldn't seem to get my heart rate under control. I could feel my heart beating out of my chest. Imagine the first time a boy sent shivers up your spine. Now multiply that by a thousand. I experienced one shiver after another for hours.

Somehow, I wrote the essay assigned, the question being, "Do I agree with this quote by Malcolm X: 'Education is the passport to the future, for tomorrow belongs to those who prepare for it today'?" Unsure what kind of essay I put on paper, I really hoped I actually answered the question. It determined which English classes I qualified for. Really an inconvenient day for fate or destiny or whatever you would call it to show up.

Relieved that this part of orientation was over. Lunch. Rey promised answers at lunch. I couldn't even fathom what those answers might be. I didn't know if I could successfully eat anything. I had never been one to skip a meal, but there was a first time for everything. I knew if I put food in this stomach, I would have to taste it twice.

I reached over and gave Daniel a quick hug and thanked him for keeping me company. All the while, Rey had grabbed my hand and didn't let go of it while I hugged Daniel. *Possessive, is he?* I thought. It made me feel wanted in a way I had never experienced, so I couldn't find it in me to get upset with him. Daniel wished me luck and rushed off to see someone else he recognized while we were listening to the administration ramble on.

There they were again, those gorgeous chocolate brown eyes staring into mine. *"What do you want for lunch?"*

"I couldn't possibly eat anything right now."

Relief washed over him when he said, "I feel the same, but I didn't want you to go hungry." He still had my hand in his hand while we headed off together in search of a quiet place to talk.

Rey

I found it hard to believe I had spent the last few hours sitting next to the girl I believed I had lost for all eternity. I couldn't bring myself to move even an inch away from her, for fear it might all have been a dream and she would disappear from my life once again.

I couldn't bring myself to let go of her soft hand. Of course, hers was smaller than mine, making my hand fit around it like a glove. I had so many emotions for this beautiful, sexy, marvelous girl for so long. I didn't know how jealous I would feel when I saw her in the presence of another guy. It felt like someone digging sharp objects into my chest while twisting them around at the same time. I only felt relief when we moved away from the crowd and were on our own.

Next, the hard part, to explain everything to her. I could only pray she understood and wouldn't bolt.

"Do you want to sit at a table somewhere, or would the grass under those trees be all right with you?" She agreed to sit under the trees. Relieved because I could more easily touch her on the grass.

Overwhelmed with an unexplainable urge to be in constant physical contact with her. Not something my family told me to expect. I would have to ask that question, along with the burning question inside of me. *How did she speak to me today?*

We sat down together in the grass. I made sure we could see each other. I planned to talk out loud mostly, but in case I wanted to speak into her mind, I wanted to be looking into her beautiful eyes. Eyes so similar to my own, they were so dark, I could get lost in them. The way a wayward traveler would get lost in the woods on a dark, moonless night. I let go of her hand so she could sit down. Once we were sitting, I pressed my knees up against hers.

"Lisabeth, my love, my soulmate. I will start at the beginning. It would be easier for me to tell you the entire story from the beginning without interruptions. I don't want to leave anything out. I'm already so nervous. You mentioned never having been vulnerable with anyone; well, neither have I. I will answer all your questions as soon as I tell you everything."

She nodded for me to proceed.

"My ancestors were from Salem, Massachusetts. No, they were not witches. They had inquisitive minds, and it's the mind that intrigued them the most. They believed if they studied, tested, and researched the human brain, they would find secrets no one had ever found before. What they discovered is what my family termed *the soulmate call*. They found after years of tests and experiments we could tap into the part of our soul that reaches out for our mates, the other half of our souls, the one created just for us. In tapping into that part of our soul, which connects to our minds, we found we could call our soulmate by pushing our thoughts into their thoughts. If they truly are yours, their soul will hear yours and call back. I don't know exactly how they discovered this. I only know the mind exercises; these exercises are a type of meditation we pass down from generation to generation. Everyone in my family grows up doing these exercises, knowing one day we will feel an urge in our soul to call out to our other half when we meet them. When I saw you that first day at the restaurant, I felt that urge to call out to your soul. It felt exactly like everyone said it would. We're also taught to use wisdom, and not to call out until we think our other half is ready to hear it. I didn't call out to you that day. I was a stupid boy, not ready for it to be you or anyone else. Being eighteen, still young. I stupidly wanted to sow my wild oats. Not quite ready to be with someone forever. I also stupidly felt put out you were waiting for marriage. I have been a selfish, horny toad for as long as I can remember. I thought to myself I had to be wrong. It wasn't you, not this early in my life, and the girl for me definitely wouldn't expect me to wait. I ignored that pull for months. That day at my grams'. I couldn't resist the urge to call your soul for a moment longer, but you didn't answer. My heart broke when I didn't hear you say anything. That's what moved me to tears that day. An indescribable pain I had never felt before became more than I could bear. By the next day, my pride began overruling my love for you. I told myself I would try one more time, and if you didn't answer, then I would say goodbye and never look back. I did. I called your soul once more in my truck. When you didn't respond, I became so angry. Angry at myself for falling for you, angry because I thought I must have misread my urges, and angry at you for not hearing me. When I told my grams what happened, she slapped me in the back of my head. Called me a stupid idiot even. She explained to me where I went wrong with us is I didn't win your heart first. Not until the heart of the person you're meant for falls for you can they hear you. This is the part the immature kid in me forgot all about. After I pushed you away, I thought I would have to live without you. Certain I would face this life alone without being complete. I kept up my relationship with my girlfriend for about another month, hoping I would forget you. The guilt and the shame of what I had done became too much for me. I broke up with her and haven't seen or dated anyone since. Ironically, I agreed to a blind date tonight. My friends have been nagging me for months. I said yes to get it over with. I will definitely cancel that date. I would prefer to spend my evening taking you on our first proper date. I'm confused. I heard your voice today before I called out to you again. I don't know how you did that. It has become the happiest moment of my life when you did. All the pain and anguish I have been feeling immediately lifted right off of my shoulders. I have been talking so fast I have barely given myself a chance to breathe. I want you to be my girl and I want to be your guy. I understand you may need some time, and I will wait forever if I must. I'm going to shut up now to give you a chance to ask me questions or to slap me in the face. Whatever you need."

Lisabeth

I sat there listening to the unbelievable tale, and I couldn't bring myself to doubt any of it. I knew what he said about us being soulmates to be true. I felt it; the pull so powerfully strong it felt tangible. I couldn't say I understood how this "soulmate call" worked, but I knew it happened. *Am I ready for this?* I thought to myself.

Rey didn't fit the picture of the type of guy I planned on bringing home to my parents. The guy you brought home to my parents needed to be a church guy. I didn't know how to introduce him to my family.

He bared his soul to me. Was it possible to fall in love with someone again? Then I did. I fought back tears; I don't even know what kind of tears they were. They weren't tears of sadness or joy. They were just tears. Tears of an emotion I didn't know how to describe yet. He finished telling me about *the soulmate call* when a tear slipped past my control and slid down my cheek. He did the perfect thing and brushed it away with his thumb.

How should I respond to this man? Yes, he had moved from the boy I met over a year ago to a man. A man ready to commit, ready to love, ready for a happily ever after. He grew up while we were apart.

I saw him waiting for me to say something. He probably heard everything I thought anyway, so where should I start? Still not ready to open myself up for him to see inside of me entirely. I looked away for a moment to gather myself without the risk of him hearing everything that crossed my mind.

He sat by me, being extremely patient, waiting for me to speak. I started slowly with what I had to say, refusing to look directly at him. "I believe you. I don't fully understand what has happened, but I get it happened." The pull to each other became too intense. I couldn't continue to look away.

I used our connection to continue because hearing my voice admit what I felt seemed like too much too soon. *"I believe you. When I first saw you, I felt my soul reach out to yours and connect. Like pushing a plug into an outlet. And then the electricity flowed from my soul to yours. I didn't know how to describe it, but I felt it. I can't deny what I felt and what is happening. I feel our souls tying together. I'm unprepared for all of this, but I'm not running from it. I don't know where we go from here, but I will go with you."*

"What am I going to tell my parents? They won't approve of you."

Rey opened his mouth for the first time since I began my response. "How do you know they won't like me? What about me would make them not give me a chance?"

One word sealed my explanation: "Church." I then looked away, actually ashamed they might very well reject this man, my soulmate, the one created for me.

He gently grabbed my chin and turned my face to look at him. *"I can go to church for them. I can even become a Jesus freak for you. Whatever you need from me. I won't be the one that causes you pain if I can help it. This is a minor hurdle we can climb over together. If you will let me."*

Again, I felt the tears coming. I could only describe them as tears of love. It's not joy or sadness I felt. I could only describe the feeling as a blanket of emotion covering me in strength and peace. I saw that big grin on his face, and I knew I forgot to look away. Would I ever get used to this?

"Probably not anytime soon, and I won't complain." Rey teased before asking me, "Will you do me the honor of allowing me to take you out on an actual date tonight?"

"Yes, I would love to. There is nothing else I would rather do tonight."

The next thing I knew, he leaned in and gently brushed his lips against mine. It sounded like someone had lit fireworks in the background. "Breathe, Lisabeth, breathe," I heard Rey saying, his voice pulling my head back into focus.

We noticed everyone around moving to gather. It must have been time for our tour of the campus. My major was English with the Liberal Arts Department, and his major was Computer Technology with the Technology Department. This meant we had to go our separate ways for now.

"Meet me right back here after the tour, please. We can make plans for tonight, then."

I assured him I would be there. He helped me to my feet, then he again leaned in and brushed his lips against mine. Now I had to figure out how to walk without falling from the weakness in my knees. He grinned at me with those dimples. I remembered he could hear me.

"See you soon, my beautiful, brown-eyed girl," he told me before parting ways for now.

**The full version of The Soulmate Call is free
to download on Kindle & iBooks.**

Made in the USA
Columbia, SC
12 July 2022

63341893R00134